There was a table right in the middle of the room, a chair by it, and nothing else at all. Except a box on the table. Sig crossed to look at it.

Velvety dust all over, which he smeared away quickly. Then the flashlight picked up bright colors, so bright they seemed to glitter. There was a picture, or rather four pictures, for the top of the box was quartered into four sections. And the pictures—were pictures of dragons!

The dragon at the top was a silvery color and it had wings. It was holding up its clawed forefeet as if it were going to attack. Its red tongue, which was forked at the end like a snake's, stuck straight out of its mouth, and its green eyes stared directly at Sig.

ANDRE NORTON, one of Ace Books' most prolific writers, has turned out in DRAGON MAGIC one of the most thrilling of her many tales.

Miss Norton is a resident of Florida.

DRAGON MAGIC

by Andre Norton

A Tempo Star Book

Distributed by Ace Books
Grosset & Dunlap, Inc., Publishers
New York, N.Y. 10010
A Filmways Company

Dedication:

For Anne McCaffrey and
L. Sprague de Camp,
two notable tamers of dragons

DRAGON MAGIC

Copyright © 1972 by Andre Norton
A Tempo Star Book, by arrangement with
Thomas Y. Crowell Company
All Rights Reserved
ISBN: 0-441-16644-X

First Ace printing: May, 1973
Second Ace printing: February, 1980

Printed in U.S.A.

CONTENTS

1

HIDDEN TREASURE

Sig Dortmund kicked at a pile of leaves in the gutter, watched the crowd at the school bus stop. With just one bus running from this new development, they picked up the little kids, too. Just a few guys here his age. Yeah, only three. And this was a double run, to the elementary and to the middle school—you had to leave a lot earlier in the morning and get home when it was too late to do anything outside. Swell year this was going to be! He kicked harder.

Those three guys, he tried to look them over without them seeing him do it. Well, he sort of knew the small one. He'd been in social studies with him last year. What was his name? Artie—Artie Jones. Should he say "Hi, Artie?"

Artie Jones chewed on his lower lip. What a jam this was. All the little kids shoving and yelling. Bet everyone would be good and deaf before they let them off at elementary. And look what he had to maybe sit with! There was that big guy—he'd seen him last term, but he was no "big man," that was for sure. Then take that Chinese kid over by the wall. Mom had heard all about him. She told them at supper last night. How Mr. Stevens had been in Vietnam and had gone to Hong Kong on leave. There he ran across this Kim in an orphanage and wanted to adopt him. The Stevenses had to wait a long time to bring him over, even had to get their congressman in on the deal. Didn't look as if he was worth all that bother, did he?

9

They said he was bright in school. But of course the Stevenses would brag about him after taking all that trouble to get him here. Big deal—jokers like him to ride with!

Kim Stevens held tightly to his book bag. All the noise and confusion! He had heard plenty of noise, been caught in crowds of people ever since he could remember. Hong Kong was so crowded that people lived on top of people there. But that was different. Those had been his people, he *knew* what they were like. Last year here had been so different, too. Father had driven him to school. Yes, he had felt strange at first, but later there had been James Fong and Sam Lewis. He glanced once at the tall black boy leaning against the wall around the old house. But that one acted as if he were all alone, not even noticing the second graders almost jumping on his toes.

Ras was not listening to the noise. He had to concentrate just like Shaka said—remember and get it right. When they asked him his name he wasn't to say "George Brown"; he was to say "Ras." Just like his brother was now Shaka, not Lloyd, named after the Zulu king in Africa, the one who really gave it to whitey back in the old days. Ras meant "prince"; Shaka let him pick it out himself from the list. Shaka was sure right in the groove, he wore his hair Afro and everything.

Dad and Mom did not understand. They were old days, take all the mean things whitey wants to hand out and keep your mouth shut. Shaka, he told it like it was now. And Ras wasn't going to let anyone talk him out of doing just like Shaka said.

More leaves blew around the corner of the wall, and Sig crackled through them with a deliberate crunching. Back there was the old house they were going to tear down. He'd like to go and take a look at it, anything better than hanging around with a bunch of guys who wouldn't give you even a look, let alone the time of day. But the bus was coming.

The day, which had begun sourly, didn't get any better; sometimes they don't. At four Ras slouched again in the bus seat for the trip back home. Troublemaker, huh? He'd heard old Keefer talking. Anyway he hadn't told them anything but Ras. Not his fault Ben Crane spoke up that way. Ben—he was what Shaka called an "Uncle Tom," smoothing up whitey. Maybe Shaka could get Ras out of this dumb school into the Afro-studies one. No one to go around with. He scowled at the seat ahead.

Kim sat still, his book bag across his knees. Why didn't that boy want to tell the teacher his name? And what kind of a name was "Ras"? He just didn't understand anything in this new school. It was too big and they hurried you all the time. His head ached. He didn't belong here. Dared he say so to Father, maybe get to go back where he had been before?

Artie scuffed his feet on the bus floor. Used his eyes and ears all right today, he had. That Greg Ross was the big man in the class—played football, a cinch for the student council when they had the election the homeroom teacher gabbed about. Get into Greg's crowd and you had it made. Too bad he was too small and light for football. But he'd figure out some way to make Greg know he was around. No other way to really make it but be in that gang—outside you were nothing.

Sig, sitting next to Artie, wondered what he was thinking about. Just those three guys in his neighborhood. Artie sure wasn't very friendly—it didn't matter much about the other two. School was too big. You got lost. Artie had been in social studies and in math. But both times he pushed in to sit near that Greg Ross, like he was trying to make Ross notice him. And that Ras—not telling his real name. Get mixed up with a kook like that and, man, you might be in real trouble.

That other one—where'd he get a name like Stevens? He was Chinese or something. Never opened his mouth in the two classes where Sig had seen him. Acted like he was afraid of his own shadow. Sure going to be some drag, riding with this bunch all year.

As the bus swung in to drop them at the corner, Sig noticed something different. The gates guarding the old house were gone, bushes broken down inside as if some truck had pulled in and out. He had heard they were going to tear the house down, make another parking lot there.

Sig lingered as the first wave of children swept on down the street. It sure looked spooky in there. He remembered that some old guy had lived there for a long time. Wouldn't sell the place even when they offered him a lot of money. He'd been a kook, too, from what Dad said—lived in other countries digging up old bones and things belonging to people back in history.

Last year when their class at the other school had gone on a museum trip, Miss Collins had shown them things in the Egypt room and the China room that the old man had given to the city. And when he had died there had been a long piece about him in the paper. Mom had read it out loud. She was interested because she knew Mrs. Chandler, who used to go in and clean house for him once in awhile. He kept some rooms locked up, though, and she never saw what was in those.

What had he kept locked up? Treasure, maybe—things he had found in old tombs and such places. What had happened to them when he died? Did they take them all to the museum?

Sig balanced from one foot to the other a pace inside the wall, standing on the weedy, overgrown drive. He wouldn't like to come here after dark. But what about those locked rooms? Suppose they were still locked and everyone had forgotten about them? Suppose you could get inside and really find—

A shiver ran up Sig's back. You could find a treasure! Why, then you could buy a bike, or a real official league baseball and bat— He had a list of things he dreamed of owning some day. If he had any of those, you bet the guys would notice him, even in a big school like Anthony Wayne! To find a treasure!

Only, a big, dark place like that—Sig didn't want to go poking around in there alone. It got dark fast now, and they were bussed home so late. He'd need someone else to go along, but Artie was the only possibility. Suppose he asked him about it? Told him about the locked rooms and the treasure? That would wake him up all right, make him know that there were other people in the world besides Greg Ross. Artie'd really listen to Sig if he had something like that to say. Just wait until tomorrow!

However, it was hard to corner Artie long enough to talk to him alone, as Sig discovered the next day. In the first place Artie was late in reaching the bus stop, getting in just before the bus pulled out, and so sitting at the very front. And he was off and away before Sig could catch up with him. But at homeroom time Sig got him by the arm.

"Listen"—he made it fast because Artie was pulling against his hold, looking beyond Sig to where the Ross guy and those fellows he ran around with were in a huddle—"listen, Artie, I've got to tell you something important—"

Now Ross went up to talk to Mr. Evans and Artie relaxed, looked at Sig as if he had just seen him.

"What?" His tone was impatient.

"You know that big old house, the one they are going to tear down, the one at the corner?"

"Sure. What's so important about that?"

Artie was again trying to look around Sig. But Sig planted himself firmly before the smaller boy, intent on gaining his interest.

"My mom knows a lady who used to work there. She said that the old guy who owned it kept some rooms locked up, wouldn't ever let her look in them. You remember last year when we went to the museum and they showed us all those old things he gave them—the things out of tombs he dug up in different places? Maybe he didn't give them all away, maybe some are still in those locked rooms. Treasure, Artie!"

"You're crazy. They wouldn't be left there now, not when the whole house is going to be torn down." But Artie was looking at Sig now, was listening. "You ought to know that!"

"I asked Mom this morning. She said nobody had been inside much since the old guy died. The lawyer said all the things inside were to go to the Good Will people, but they haven't come yet to haul them away. Mrs. Chandler has the house keys and nobody's asked for them. So that means maybe something's still there."

"If it's all locked up, how are you going to get in?"

Sig grinned. "There're ways." He was not quite sure what ways, but he would not tell Artie that. The more he thought about it, the more he was sure that there was treasure just waiting to be found. And it would not hurt anyone to take it. The old guy did not have any family. And if it was all just going to be given to the Good Will—

14

"When are you going to do it?" Artie had stopped fidgeting so much, was listening carefully now.

"I brought a flashlight. We'd better try today. Don't know when the Good Will people will come. The gates were taken off yesterday, they must be getting ready to tear the place down soon. We may not have much time."

"All right," Artie agreed just as the bell rang. "After school."

Artie hurried quickly to the seat just behind Greg Ross. Sig went to his own place in the back row. As he turned he bumped into Ras. Had he been listening? Sig frowned down at his math book. The treasure seemed more real every minute he thought about it. If that Ras had an idea he was going to muscle in—well, Artie and he would be two against one, so he had better not try anything, he had just better not!

Ras sat down. Treasure in the old house? Shaka was always talking about how they needed money for the Cause, a lot of money. Suppose, suppose Ras could find this treasure, give it to Shaka. Then he would be helping out. Treasure in the old house, and those two were going after it tonight. There was no reason why Ras could not trail along behind them, see just what they were doing or what they found, no reason at all.

Sig and Artie slid out of the bus toward the end of the crowd getting out at the corner that afternoon. They wanted to be the last to leave, and so stood talking at the break in the wall where the gates had been torn out until the rest of the children were gone.

"O.K. to go in now." Artie sounded as impatient as he had earlier. "My mom will be wondering why I don't get home if she sees the rest of the kids going by."

Sig hesitated. Now that the time had actually come he

liked his idea a little less. The bushes grew tall and hung over the drive that was almost hidden. It had been cloudy all day, though it had not yet rained, and that made it look very dark in there.

"Well, are you coming or aren't you? Big talk about treasure. You afraid or something?" Artie, several paces farther up the drive, turned around.

"I'm coming, I'm coming, all right!" Sig had the big camping flashlight out and ready in his hand.

The drive led around the side of the house to the back, where there were some other buildings strung out. They looked as if they were all falling apart. The roof was off the end of one. But the house was in good condition, even the windows unbroken.

"Where do we get in at?" Artie asked impatiently.

There was a door at the side, which turned out to be locked. There was another in the back, opening off a small, screened-in porch. But the screening was rusty and had holes in it. Sig pulled at a piece and it tore right off in his hand. The door there also was locked, but there were two windows, one on either side.

"You hold this!" Sig thrust the flashlight into Artie's hand, dropped his book bag on the porch, and tried the nearer window. He was not going to let Artie think he was afraid, not when it was his own plan.

At first the window would not budge; then it moved, but so hard that Artie had to help him push it up. There was a queer smell from inside. Sig sniffed and did not like it. But they could enter, and that was what mattered —he had proved this much to Artie.

They climbed over the sill and Sig switched on the flashlight, shining it around.

"Just a kitchen," Artie said as the light picked up a sink, a very large stove that did not look much like those they had in the new houses, and a lot of cupboards.

"Sure," Sig answered. "What did you think it was going to be? That was the back porch, so it opens from a kitchen." Somehow the sight of that ordinary-looking sink and the stove made him feel more at home.

There were two doors. Artie opened the first to show steps leading down into the dark. He closed it hurriedly.

"Basement!"

"Yeah." Sig was gaining confidence, though he did not want to explore below. However, he was sure that Mrs. Chandler's locked rooms were not in the basement.

The other door gave into a much smaller room, which had glass-doored cupboards all around it. The glass was heavily coated with dust. Sig rubbed away a patch to look inside, but he saw nothing there except a lot of dishes.

Another door from this room brought them into a big dining room. Artie sneezed.

"Sure is dusty. Say, this is a big house. Look at the size of that table. Could feed our whole family for Thanksgiving and we have about fourteen people, counting the Grands and all. One guy, living here alone, must have felt queer with so much room."

Sig was already ahead into another dim room, where the shades were pulled down, making it a gloomy cave. The flashlight showed them tables, chairs, a sofa. Some of the furniture had been covered up with sheets, even newspapers. Beyond was a hall with two more doors. The first opened on a room with a big desk and a lot of shelves, a few books still lying on some. The next one, though, did not open to Sig's tugging. He turned excitedly to Artie.

"This is locked! Must be one of those rooms Mrs. Chandler talked about."

Artie grabbed the knob in turn, tried to open the door.

"So it's locked, so now how are you going to get it

open? Recite something to it, maybe, like that guy in the fairy tale I read to my sister last night." Artie stepped back, threw up his hands as if he were about to perform some feat of magic, and said in a deep voice, "Open, sesame!"

"You wait, you just wait!" Sig could not be defeated, not now, not with Artie grinning at him that way. He ran back to the front room and got a poker he had seen by the fireplace. But when he brought it back Artie looked surprised—not only surprised but frightened.

"Now look here, Sig, you go breaking things up and you'll be in bad trouble. There were a couple of guys I heard about that got into a house and broke up stuff. And then they were arrested, and their folks had to go down to the police station and get them. I don't want any part of breaking stuff up. It's late, my mom will be wondering where I am. I'm going right now!"

"Go on," Sig retorted. "Go on. You won't get any of the treasure."

"There's no treasure, anyway. And you're just asking for trouble, Sig Dortmund!"

Artie turned and ran. For a moment Sig was ready to follow him. Then, stubbornly, he went back to the door. There was a treasure, he knew there was. And he would have it all to himself now. Let Artie beat it; Artie was chicken.

Sig raised the poker awkwardly, but when he touched the door it just swung right open. It was not locked, after all. He dropped the poker, to use the flashlight. There were two windows, but they had shutters closed tightly across them. Sig had never seen shutters *inside* a house before. Usually they were hung for trimming on the outside. In fact, he had not known they could be closed. There was a table right in the middle of the room, a chair by it, and nothing else at all. Except a box on the table. Sig crossed to look at it.

Velvety dust all over, which he smeared away quickly. Then the flashlight picked up bright colors, so bright they seemed to glitter. There was a picture, or rather four pictures, for the top of the box was quartered into four sections. And the pictures—were pictures of dragons!

The dragon at the top was a silvery color and it had wings. It was holding up its clawed forefeet as if it were going to attack. Its red tongue, which was forked at the end like a snake's, stuck straight out of its mouth, and its green eyes stared directly at Sig.

To the left below was a red dragon with a long tail which curled up and over its back, ending in an arrow point. The right-hand dragon was coiled up as if asleep, its big head resting on its paws, its eyes closed. It was yellow. The dragon at the bottom had the queerest of shapes. Its body was more like an an animal's, with paws in front but hind feet like big bird claws. Its neck was long and held high, and its head was small, like a snake's. It was blue in color.

Sig opened the box and his surprise was complete. It was full to the brim with parts of a jigsaw puzzle, queer-shaped bits all tumbled together. Except that they were so brightly colored, they glittered almost as if they were, indeed, diamonds, emeralds, rubies. Sig ran his fingers through the jumble of pieces and snatched them away. They had felt—queer! And yet now he wanted to touch them again.

He put the lid back on the box and picked it up, holding it close to him. He could not take it home, there would be too many questions asked. But he was going to keep it; he had found it after Artie had gone, so Artie had no claim on it.

But Artie was right about one thing—it was getting late. He would just hide this and come back tomorrow to look it over. Also, he had not explored the rest of the house.

Hide it—where? There were all those covers in the other room. Suppose Artie came back on his own or told someone? This was Sig's treasure and he was going to keep it!

Sig crossed the hall and slipped the box under one of the sheeting covers. He left the door of the other room half ajar as he made his way out of the house. As he hurried down the drive he did not see that shadow within a shadow by the half-dead lilac bush.

2

FAFNIR

Sig hung back at the bus stop the next morning, not wanting any questions from Artie. But when he got on the bus Artie was not there, and he settled down in a seat a little uneasily. Suppose Artie had told someone? He tried not to think about what Artie might have done or been doing. But when Artie was not in first-period class, and didn't show up in math, either, Sig's uneasiness grew. He had been dumb, letting Artie in on the secret at all. Tonight he would get the dragon box out of the house. Then—

The rest of the day was disaster added to disaster as far as Sig was concerned. There was a test in math, to see how well they had remembered things over vacation. And Sig discovered that he did not even know what some of the questions meant. Mr. Bevans had never taught them anything like that back at the Lakemount School.

And in the cafeteria—well, it was no fun eating alone. Everyone else in the whole place either was part of a crowd or else had at least one other guy to sit with. Except kooks like that Stevens kid and that Ras. They sat alone, but Sig was sure not going to join either one of them. Artie had not shown up, either, which meant he had not come to school today.

The afternoon dragged on and on. Sig thought it was never going to end. But at last he tramped back to his locker, stuck his math book and his social studies notebook into his book bag, and went for the bus. Five problems in math—and he still did not understand how you were supposed to work them. This Mr. Sampson sure was tough, and he thought you ought to get it right the first time when he scribbled something on the board and said real fast "This is . . ." and "That is . . ." Then he would look around and snap "Understand?" But his voice made it plain that he expected you to say "yes" whether you did or not. And Sig knew he did not.

He was no brain, he had always known that. But if he were given time and someone would go over it with him —well, he had not done too badly at Lakemount. Only everything had not been such hurry, hurry there as it was here at Anthony Wayne. He stared glumly out of the window and wondered if the whole year was going to be this way.

Ras balanced his big notebook on his knee and watched Sig in short, stolen glances from time to time. What had the big boy and Artie been doing in that old house last night? And why had Artie come out in such a hurry while Sig stayed in? Ras had not told Shaka about it yet. But now he wondered. Suppose they did something in the house to bring the police—who would be blamed? Ras nodded. Always the same thing, Shaka said. When the police looked around for somebody to blame for something, they picked out a black man first. Should he be bright and stay away, or should he follow Sig if he went in the house tonight? But why had Sig stayed last night after Artie came out in such a hurry? Ras had to know the reason for that. Yes, he would follow Sig if he went in there again.

Kim sat with his eyes on his book bag. Inside he felt lost and empty, almost as bad as he had in Hong Kong after the old woman had died and left him on his own.

He had never known whether she was his grandmother or not. Sometimes she said she was, other times she had yelled mean things at him, called him a toad-faced nothing. But at least she had known he was alive. After she died there had been no one, not until he had gone to the mission one day, tagging behind some other boys hoping for a bowl of noodles.

And he had been fed. After that, things changed. First he stayed in the mission orphanage. Then he met Father, and came to America. But now he felt alone again, with no one caring at school, as if he, Kim Stevens, were not even there. Sometimes he felt as if he were invisible, like those demons the old woman used to frighten him with. What if he could turn into a demon, one of the red-faced monsters he had seen pictured on a temple wall? And did it right in class? They would know who he was then!

Should he go and pick up the dragon box tonight? Sig wondered. He wished he knew what had happened to Artie, if he had told anyone about last night. But supposing the Good Will people came soon to take everything out of the house? Yes, he had better get the box tonight and find someplace to hide it. But why did he want it so badly? Sig was a little puzzled about his own feeling. He had never cared much for jigsaw puzzles before. Well, somehow this was different. And he knew that he had to have it.

He would do as they had last night, wait until the kids scattered away from the bus stop and then go in and get the box. He did not like the idea of being in the house alone, though. The rooms were so big and dark. And he had not brought the flashlight.

There were a lot of clouds, too. He would have to hurry to get home before the rain started. Or Mom would ask some questions harder to answer than the math ones were today. Luckily Sig could remember right where he had left the box, under a piece of sheeting on the seat of a small couch.

The bus was taking a lot of time, all those stops to let kids off. Sig kicked his heels against the floor and wished he could get out and run. That way he might get there sooner.

It was so cloudy when the bus finally reached his corner that Sig knew he dared not try to go to the house. Artie—thinking of Artie gave him a new plan. It was almost as if someone had told him what to do, step by step. He was so pleased with his new idea that he did not stop to think past putting it into action. He made his way straight home.

As he went through his front door he felt a twinge of uneasiness. What he was going to tell Mom was not exactly true. But it might be the only chance for him to get the dragon box. And he had to take it.

"Mom?" There was no answer to his call. Sig went on to the kitchen.

On the table was a plate of cookies. As Sig reached for one he saw the note held down under the edge of the plate. Mom was not here, she had gone to Aunt Kate's. There would be an hour, maybe more, before Dad got home. So he would not have to tell the made-up story about taking Artie's homework to him. He could easily get the box and no one would know.

Cramming another cookie into his mouth, Sig got his flashlight and pulled on his slicker. It was already raining. All the better, nobody would be hanging around to see him go to the house.

He felt excited at the adventure and now he was glad to be alone. He bet that Artie, or Greg Ross, even, would be afraid to go into the house by himself in the dark. But he, Sig Dortmund, was not.

Many more leaves had piled up in the drive of the old house, and the rain plastered them to the broken concrete. Sig edged around to the back porch. It was harder getting the window up without Artie to help him. He propped it up with a loose brick from the back steps. Then he hurried across the kitchen, pantry, dark dining room, to the parlor where he had left the dragon box.

Only, the sheet cover was flipped back and the box was gone!

Artie! Sig felt hot with anger. Artie had come and taken it away. His hand clenched into a fist. He was not going to let Artie get away with this. It was his box, he had found it after Artie had left. Artie was going to give it back!

Sig paused in the hall. How had Artie known about the box? Maybe—maybe Artie had only pretended to go, had hidden somewhere and watched him, had planned to take the box as soon as he was gone! Well, Artie was going to give it back, if Sig had to go to his house to make him do it.

But Sig froze. A sound, a scraping sound. It had come from the room where he had found the box. Artie! Maybe Artie was still here and he could catch him!

Sig tiptoed down the hall to the half-open door. Artie could not have expected Sig or he would have hidden. So Sig could surprise him—

He paused by the door. The room was lighter than it had been yesterday. One of the shutters which crossed the window had been opened. And there he was by the table with the box!

"Got you!" Sig pressed the button on the flashlight and the ray caught that figure.

Only it was not Artie at all. It was that Ras guy. But he did have the box. Its lid was open and some of the pieces were spilled out on the tabletop. Of all the nerve!

"Give me that!" Sig moved quickly. "That's mine! What do you think you're doing?"

"Yours?" Ras grinned and Sig did not like that grin, nor the tone of his voice as he added, "Who gave it to you? Finders keepers."

"It's mine!" Somehow getting that box into his own hands again seemed to Sig the most important thing in the world. But before he could grab it Ras snatched it away, so that a lot of the pieces inside sifted over the rim and fell out on the dusty tabletop. Their bright colors sparkled as if they really were jewel stones, so brilliantly they glowed.

"Yours?" Ras repeated. "I don't think so. I think you found it here and now you want to steal it. Yeah, steal it! It belongs to whoever owns this house, not to you. Isn't that true now? You stole it, whitey. Just like your kind steal a lot of things. My brother, he's got the right of it, whitey. Your kind aren't any good."

Ras deliberately shook the box again and a sprinkling of pieces fell over its edge. Sig cried out and tried to jerk the box out of Ras's hold, but the other boy eluded him easily. Then Sig threw away the flashlight and launched himself in a tackle. He was clumsy, but he brought Ras down and the other dropped the box to defend himself.

Sig had been in fights before, but this was more real than any of those. It seemed as if Ras wanted to hurt, and Sig discovered that he wanted to hurt back. But, though they flailed at each other, few of the blows found their mark. However, Sig's determined advance did herd Ras into the hall. Then that hot fury, which had been building in Sig ever since he had discovered the box missing, boiled over and he jumped at Ras in a blind rage.

The other ran, as if something about Sig had suddenly frightened him so that he just wanted to get away. They crossed the hall, ran through the dark rooms. In the dining room Sig ran straight into a chair that Ras had pushed out in his path. He fell, and when he got to his feet again some of the anger was gone. But he still kept on. When he reached the kitchen Ras was already at the window, trying to get that stubborn pane up farther.

Sig sprang and caught handfuls of jacket near the other's shoulders.

"No you don't!" He tried to pull Ras back, though the boy held fast to the windowsill.

Then, outside, there was a vivid stroke on lightning, as startling as if it had struck the old house. Ras let go his hold, frightened by that flash in his very face. Sig staggered back from the window, pulling him along.

Ras jerked and pulled, wriggling free of Sig's hold. But, as if he had been confused by the lightning, he now headed not back to the window but across the kitchen to the basement door. And he was gone through that before Sig could move.

Sig sat up. When Ras had pulled free he had overbalanced and landed on the floor. The door banged shut behind Ras. Sig looked around the kitchen. He had to get the box and pick up all those pieces Ras had dropped on the table and floor. But if he left the kitchen Ras could get out and go and tell—or else he would start fighting again for the box.

Sig got to his feet, sore in all those places which had hit the chair in the dining room. He limped to the table and began to push it across the dusty floor. It was big and heavy and hard to move, but at last he got it jammed against the basement door. Now Ras could just stay down there until he, Sig, was ready to let him out. And he would make him promise some things first.

Dimly Sig felt odd, as if this were not he, Sig Dortmund, who made such plans or did such things. As if something else or someone else had gotten into his body. But that was silly—it could not happen. No, he was Sig Dortmund, and he was going to get his box. It was *his* box! Then he would settle with Ras.

He went back to the other room. His flashlight, still turned on, had rolled back against the wall, the light a path across the floor. Sparkling in that light were a lot of the jigsaw pieces. The box lay on its side where the rest of the pieces had spilled out. Sig caught it up hurriedly to make sure it was not broken. If Ras had hurt it any—!

But it was all right. He began picking up its contents, restoring them as fast as he could. They felt smooth, and their colors were so bright. He cupped a handful, red, green, silver—the silver ones must be for the top dragon in the picture. And this red—for the red dragon, probably—and the blue—the yellow—

He had gathered up all the pieces on the floor now, using the flashlight to search carefully, make sure he had not overlooked any. Some of the bits were pretty small and it would be easy to lose one. He even got down and crawled around on his hands and knees, stirring up dust enough to make himself cough. But at last he was sure he had them all.

There were more on the table. And how much time did he have? Dad would be home soon, and if he wasn't there—well, there would be a lot of questions. He would just sweep the pieces carefully into the box now.

But when Sig straightened up to do that his hand moved slower and slower, and he stared at what lay there. He had seen puzzles before, only this one was different. Three of the sparkling silver pieces were already stuck together. They must be part of the silver dragon. And here was another bit. Yes, and it fitted in right there!

Sig sat down on the waiting chair, dumped out the box he had so recently filled, and began to hunt for silver bits, as if nothing else in the world mattered. Though the room was dark he did not need any light, because the pieces appeared to have a light of their own. Not only that, but as he fitted them together and the right ones touched, the light grew brighter. But to Sig that did not seem in the least odd.

Nor was he aware of time passing as his fingers combed through the piles of pieces to separate all those of silver, toppling the rest back into the box. For he was now intent on one thing, the putting together of the dragon. He *had* to see it complete.

Touch told him that this puzzle was far thicker than the ones he had known before, being mounted on wood. The reverse sides of the pieces had strange black marks across them which could be printing, except they did not form any word he had ever seen. They were like rows of small, irregular twigs. And when he looked at them closely they made his eyes feel queer, and he turned them over again, picture side up, hurriedly.

Silver bits. Sig checked through the box again, making sure he had them all, and then he went to work. Sometimes he was lucky and a whole section went together quickly. Other times he had to hunt and hunt for one missing piece. Then it might turn out to be not the shape he thought it would be at all.

Outside, rain lashed against the windows and walls of the old house. There were more lightning flashes, and the heavy rumble of thunder. But Sig no longer noticed the storm. He had the wings of the dragon, its back, now put together; there was one hind leg ready to join on. Yes, here was the connecting piece for that.

The head came last and was the hardest. Some pieces seemed to be missing and Sig searched with growing uneasiness. He again studied the picture on the box cover and realized that the dragon was not all silver, after all.

It had red eyes and a red tongue, and there were greenish bits here and there. With haste Sig raked through the box again.

Red bits, green bits—But there was so much red and green in the box! Some pieces fell out on the floor and Sig had to get down with the flashlight to hunt them. But at last he had some which seemed possible.

He put in a piece with a blazing eye and blaze it did, almost as if it were watching him! Sig wiped the hand which had fitted in that bit across the front of his jacket. The piece had a queer feel, almost slippery. He did not like it. But the fascination of finishing the dragon held him. Now a green bit which formed a curved horn on the dragon's nose. Yes, and here was the tongue, or part of it. Again his fingers selected the right pieces as if he knew just where they lay.

There it was—no, not quite. When he compared the puzzle to the dragon of the picture one tiny piece was missing. It was the forked tongue end, raised and thrust out of the dragon's open mouth like a spear. Why had he thought of it like that?

Sig turned over the boxed pieces. Just one tongue tip. Surely it was not lost! He had to find it.

Then he saw a piece wrong side up, showing those lines of black sticks like writing. Sig turned it over and it went neatly into place.

He leaned back in the chair. The need to get the picture together no longer drove him. A dragon—a big silver dragon all ready to claw, bite—and kill.

A dragon—Fafnir—

Who—what—was Fafnir? One part of Sig cried that question against a chill, cold fear. Another part of him knew.

The dragon coiled, reared. Sig could smell a nasty odor. The coiling dragon was turning around and around, turning so fast that sparks flew from its silver scales. Sig could hear a pounding and a loud, clanging noise.

SIG CLAWHAND

There was a cold wind coming from the craigs, cold enough to pierce swordlike to the very bones under one's smoke-grimed skin. Sig Clawhand shivered, but still he drew no closer to the warmth of the forge, where sparks flew like fiery rain and the clang-clang of the smith's hammer made a noise to deafen watchers. No one watched today, though, by Mimir Master-Smith's own orders. For it was Sigurd King's-Son who wrought with that hammer against metal of his own choosing to make a sword—such a sword as would cut through the armor of Amiliar.

Sig Clawhand rubbed the twisted fingers which had given him that hard name against his thin chest. Under the loose coat of shag-wolf hide he scratched skin so long dusted with charcoal that sometimes he might be thought more forest troll than true son of man. All had heard much of the armor of Amiliar, that anyone who strode the land with it on his back, across his chest, need fear no spear, no sword forged by any mortal man. And so loudly had those boasts rung across the world that Mimir (who, men said, was of the old dwarfish blood, of those who had worked metal for the heroes of Asgard) had frowned and blown out his lips, spoken harsh words right and left, until all his roof had felt the knife edge of his tongue.

Then he had lifted up his voice in turn and sworn that he could in truth forge a blade to show Amiliar that he was not the first smith in the world, no, nor perhaps even the second! And the King of the Burgundians had laid a heavy wager upon the outcome of such a trial.

But Mimir himself was not busy at that forge, for he had Foresight. And he had laid it upon Sigurd King's-Son to do this thing. Seven days and seven nights had Sigurd worked upon the metal, and then he had taken a blade to the stream which flowed from the foot of the craig. There Mimir had set a thread of wool afloat and Sigurd had held the blade in the water so that the thread was current-driven against it—and the thread had been cleanly cut. Then all who labored in the forge shouted aloud. But Sigurd King's-Son and Mimir had looked into each other's eyes. And Sigurd had taken back the blade, had broken it into bits, to be once more heated, shaped, and tried.

He then tempered it in new-drawn milk. And he also used oatmeal, which, as all swordsmiths knew, gave strength to metal even as it did to man. Three days more he worked. Then he took what he had wrought to the stream and this time he cut with it a ball of wool without disturbing the winding of its threads.

Only, again he and Mimir exchanged looks. And Sigurd raised high the blade above a rock and brought it down with true warrior's brawn of arm so that it shattered. He then took up the bits and went once more to the forge. But that had been morn and now it was night dusk. And it was plain to Sig Clawhand that Sigurd's hammer now fell slower and with less force. And he saw the droop of Sigurd's shoulders and knew that Mimir strode back and forth by that spring of water which men said gave great knowledge to those daring to drink of it.

The wind blew cold again, and it was the cold of winter instead of, rightfully, the freshness of spring. So Sig Clawhand bunched together, his arms about his upthrust knees, making a ball of himself. He longed for the warmth of the forge side, but he knew better than to seek it now.

Then he saw two feet standing just at the level of his eyes as he curled so. Those feet wore the rough-finished hide of journey boots. As he raised his head slowly, he saw a kirtle of the same color as the sky when a storm draws near, and the sweep of a gray cloak. Higher still he looked, to a hood which was blue and which overhung a dark face. And in that face was a single eye for seeing, the other being covered with a patch of linen stuff. Yet that one eye saw into Sig so that he wished to run from it, only the power of that figure held him where he was, shivering even more than when the icy wind reached him.

"Go to Sigurd King's-Son and bid him come out. There is one here who will speak with him."

Though the stranger's voice was low there was no denying the order it gave. Sig got to his feet quickly and backed into the forge, fearing to look away from the eye which held him. Not until he was within the shadow of that doorway was he free of the bond it had laid upon him. He went to the anvil where Sigurd stood tall, the fire giving a red light to his face and his long yellow hair, looped back while he worked with tongs.

And, though he was indeed the King's son, he wore but the coarse kirtle, the leathern apron, the straw footgear which were the dress not even of a master smith but of a common laborer. Yet one looking upon him, Sig thought—any man with eyes in his head—would know this was one of kingly blood, worthy to be shield-raised when a crown was offered.

Sigurd rested the hammer against the edge of the anvil and leaned forward to see his work. But there was a frown on his tired face as if what he looked upon pleased him very little. Sig dared then to say, "Master, there is one at the door who would speak with you."

The frown was darker yet as Sigurd swung around. Sig retreated a step or two, even though Sigurd King's-Son was not one to cuff for little reason, but was kinder than most men Sig had known in his short life.

"I shall speak with no man until this task—" Sigurd King's-Son's voice was as hard as the metal he worked upon.

Then came other words which carried from the doorway. Though they did not ring as loud as Sigurd's, still one could hear them plainly.

"With me will you speak, son of Sigmund of the Volsungs!"

Sigurd King's-Son turned and stared, as did Sig also. Though the night dusk had come, yet they could plainly see the stranger as if his gray clothing and blue hood had light woven into them.

Then Sigurd dropped the hammer and went to face him, and Sig dared to follow a pace behind. This was as brave a deed as he had ever dared in his whole lifetime. For this stranger had that about him to make him seem more fearsome than Mimir.

The stranger unwrapped the fold of cloak laid about his right arm. He was carrying in the cloak pieces of dull metal. That is, they seemed dull, until the light of the forge fell upon them, and then they glittered like the small jewels Mimir set into the hilt of kings' swords.

"Son of the Volsungs, take your heritage and use it well!"

Sigurd King's-Son put forth both his hands and took the shards of metal from the stranger as if he half feared to touch what he now held, his hands even shaking a little. Sig could see that the shards were parts of a broken sword.

But the stranger was looking now at Sig, so the boy tried to raise his crooked hand to shield his face. Yet he could not complete that gesture. Rather, he had to stand under the gaze of that terrible eye.

"Let the lad lay upon the bellows in this making," said the stranger. "For there is that in this deed which is beyond the understanding of even you, Sigurd Volsung."

With that he was gone, and only the dark lay outside. He might have sunk into the ground, or taken wing into the night sky. But Sigurd was already turning back to the forge.

"Come, Sig!" Never had he said "Clawhand", for which Sig treasured each word he uttered. "This night we have much to do."

And they labored the night through, working now not with the metal from Mimir's store but rather with the broken bits the stranger had brought. Nor did Sig feel tired from what he had to do, but helped willingly in all ways as Sigurd ordered.

In the morning a blade lay ready for the testing. And it seemed to Sig that it held some of that shimmering light which had been about the hooded man in the dark. Sigurd's hand fell upon the boy's hunched shoulder.

"It is done, and done well to my thinking. We take it now for the testing."

He took up the sword and held it a little before him as a man might hold a torch to light his path. They came into the full light of day and there Mimir awaited them, the rest of his laborers and those who would learn of his skill drawn up behind him. And the Master Smith drew a hissing breath when he looked upon the blade Sigurd carried.

"So it is wrought again—Balmung, which first came from the All Father's own forge. You do well to handle it

37

with care, Sigurd King's-Son, as it once brought those of your own clan and blood to an ill end."

"Any sword can bring death to a warrior," Sigurd returned, "that is the reason for its sharp edging. But Balmung, being what it is, may now win your wager for you. To the testing—"

That testing was a mighty one, for they loosed upon the stream a whole tightly bound pack of wool, which tumbled with the current. Sigurd did not slash with the blade; rather, he stood thigh-deep in the water and held it merely in the path of the wool pack. But the wool was sliced cleanly through, so that all marveled.

Sigurd waded ashore and laid the sword carefully upon a square of fine cloth Mimir had waiting to receive it. Then he flung wide his arms and said with a laugh, "It is well said that he who yearns to make a name among men must toil for it. But it seems I have toiled overlong, master. Give me leave now to rest."

For though he was a king's son, yet in this place Sigurd acted always as one of the commoners who would learn Mimir's craft, and he asked no more than they in the way of any favor.

"It is well." Mimir nodded, busied in wrapping up the sword. "Go you to rest."

Then Sigurd turned and held out his hand to Sig. The boy had to take it awkwardly, since his right hand was the clawlike one he never willingly brought into the light.

"Here is another who has served valiantly through the night. Come you, Sig, and take the rest of a good workman." Sigurd's hand was tight upon his, drawing him on to where the laborers had their sleeping place.

"Master." Sig dragged back. "It is not well. I am but a hearth boy and there do I sleep among the ashes. See, I

38

am blackened, not fit for this place. Master Veliant and the other apprentices will be angry."

But Sigurd shook his head and continued to lead Sig. "One whom *that* stranger has set to laboring in his service need not look beneath the chin of any man when he speaks. Come now and rest."

And he made a kind of nest at the foot of his own sleeping place, so that Sig slept softer than he had for any time in his memory. Thus he became the shadow of Sigurd King's-Son. And when the other apprentices dared to speak against him, Sigurd laughed and said that it was plain Sig was a luck-bringer who should be cherished. Though the others did not like it, they dared not raise their voices against Sigurd.

But when they departed for the trial of strength against Amiliar, Sigurd took Sig apart and spoke to him, saying that the journey was long and it was best Sig stay at the forge. Sig agreed, though with a heavy heart.

He counted off the days of their absence, marking them on a smoothed stretch of earth with a stick. While they were gone he set himself a new task, that of trying to learn more of the trade so that some day perhaps he need no longer be only the hearth boy, to be cuffed and driven to the meanest of tasks. For when Sigurd left, as soon he must now, having proven his skill by the forging of Balmung, then once more Sig would be as nothing in this place.

Each day he worked to raise the heavy hammers, to try to bring them down accurately on the anvil, and each day he knew despair at his failures. But he remembered how Sigurd had worked, each time facing failure with a high head and a will to try again. And it was on the day that Sig first brought down a medium-weight hammer in a true blow that Mimir and his people returned.

They came singing, with oxcarts loaded with the fine

stuff which had been wagered and lost by the Burgundians. They told and retold the tale of how Amiliar, himself wearing his fine armor, had sat upon a hilltop and dared Mimir to prove his blade. And of how Mimir had climbed the hill, standing small indeed before Amiliar because of his dwarf blood. And of how the sword Balmung had flashed so in the sun that it had dazzled men's eyes. Then it had fallen and still Amiliar had set there. The Burgundians had raised the victory shout. But Mimir had reached forward the very tip of Balmung to touch Amiliar on the shoulder. Then his body had toppled limply, and all men could see that he had been cut asunder so cleanly that still he seemed alive, even when he was dead.

All of them praised Sigurd for the forging of such a sword. But he stood before them, shaking his head, saying that the art was by the teaching of Mimir alone—that he was the greatest swordsmith who walked the earth and the credit was his. Mimir stroked his short beard and looked pleased, ordering that a feast be made. Thereafter he shared out some of the plunder from the Burgundians to his household.

But there were those among his senior apprentices who looked with ill favor on Sigurd. They whispered among themselves that king's son though he might be, surely the King liked him little or he would not have sent him away from the court to labor as a common man at hammer and anvil. Therefore, there must be some ill hidden in him which the King knew and other men would learn to their sorrow. While they whispered thus Mimir went on one of his journeys, taking swords and spearheads and some of the Burgundian plunder to trade with the southern men who came by ship over the bitter water.

He was gone but a day when Veliant, who was senior-most among the apprentices, came to Sigurd and said, "Charcoal we have, but not enough for a long season of work. This is the time of year when we must go to the burners in the forest to renew our supplies. Mimir lets us draw lots to see who will make this journey. Come while we do so."

So they all threw bits of stone into a bowl, one such bit being scratched with Odin's sign. The bowl was given to Wulf, the cookboy, to hold as they drew without looking. Only Sig had seen Veliant talking with Wulf apart, and thereafter Wulf seemed troubled. Sig watched the drawing closely, and it seemed to him that when it came time for Sigurd to close his eyes and put forth his hand for a stone, Wulf turned and tilted the bowl a little. But this he could not prove.

However, it was the marked stone which Sigurd had to show. And though the others laughed and spoke of luck, Sig was sure that some of them nodded one to the other and smiled in an odd fashion. They made much of telling Sigurd that his was a fine journey which they all wished they might make themselves.

Sig, being uneasy in mind, crept and listened, and so heard enough to make him afraid for Sigurd. But as he was so listening, his foot moved unluckily and a branch cracked beneath him. Then hands were hard on his shoulders.

"It is the nithling!" Veliant grinned evilly at him. "How now, brothers, shall it not be as is fitting—a liege dog to lie in the King's son's grave? Since he needs must go without horse or real hound to bear him company, this shall be both! Knock him on the head!"

Those were the last words Sig heard, for a great burst of pain was in his skull and then only darkness, a darkness in which not even dreams moved. Then came pain again and Sig tried to call for help, to move, only to discover that he could not.

Afterward there was water on his face and he could see a little, though that hurt also. It was not until the pain grew less that he knew he was resting on a bed of charcoal bags, the grit of them against his cheek. He saw a fire, and by it was Sigurd. He tried to call, but his voice came only as a thin whisper of sound. But Sigurd turned quickly and came to him. He brought a drinking horn and in it a liquid of herbs which he gave to Sig sip by sip.

Thus Sig learned that they were well into the forest, and that Sigurd had been half a day on his journey before he discovered his companion, bloody-headed and trussed into the bale of empty bags loaded on the back of one of the pack donkeys. Sig warned him of the danger to come, for he was certain that Veliant thought they went to their deaths.

"Be assured we shall return," Sigurd answered. "Then there shall be an accounting between Veliant and me concerning this deed done to you. What danger can lie ahead for us when this is a journey which has been made for Mimir's forge many times?"

"But always before, master," Sig said, "it has been Mimir himself who went, never one of his men. And there are evil tales of this wood and what dwells in it."

Sigurd smiled and put his hand among the tangle of bags. From them he pulled a bundle wrapped in greased hide. With his meat knife he sawed through the lashings and stripped away the coverings to show Balmung.

"I go to no strange place without steel to my hand, forge-comrade. And with Balmung I think we have little to fear."

Sig, looking upon the sword, felt his spirits rise. For it was like a torch in the dark. He was willing to face what lay ahead, telling himself that it could hardly be worse than certain dreary days behind him.

Though the way through the forest was narrow and dark, and there was always the feeling that strange and terrifying beings watched from shadows and trailed behind them, yet they saw nothing truly to afright them. At length they came to the center of the wood to find the charcoal burners. In the open clearing they saw the dwellings of the forest men. And these men, as dark of skin from ashes and the sap of new-hewn trees as creatures of the night, snatched up weapons and stood ready to cut the travelers down. Though Sigurd wore Balmung now openly he did not draw the blade but rather called out, "Peace between us, forest men. I am of Mimir's household and I have come to buy from you under the agreement made by your master and mine."

But the leader of that wild company grinned as might a great wolf, showing teeth almost like a beast's fangs, as he answered, "You speak lies, stranger. When Mimir would deal with us he comes himself. We have our own place and no one comes into it save when we bid him. Otherwise he goes to lie beneath the All Father's tree and stares up at its branches with sightless eyes."

The men moved in a little, as do a pack of wolves when their quarry stands at bay. But before the first spear could be thrown, the first sword thrust, there came another voice: "Be not so quick for bloodshed, my dark ones. This bold man I would see."

The voice came from the large hall at the very core of the cluster of dwellings. The charcoal burners now opened their ranks to form a path for Sigurd. Sig hesitated, eyeing the forest. He wondered whether they might reach it in time by running. But with Sigurd before him, he took up the duty of a shield man, supporting his lord to the death, if that was the fate laid upon them. Trying to hold himself as straight and proud as Sigurd King's-Son, he followed after his master.

They came into the hall of the forest lord and found it to be a rich place. The high seat at the end was carved and painted, and there were weavings from the southern people on the walls. The hall was even finer than Mimir's, so that Sig stared about him round-eyed at such splendor. He thought this must be akin to the King's hall ruled over by Sigurd's father. But Sigurd looked neither to right nor left; instead he went directly to stand before the high seat where the forest lord awaited him.

The forest lord was so small that the seat seemed overlarge. One could hardly see his kirtle above the waist belt, for he had a great fan of beard reaching to his middle, while the locks on his head were long enough to mingle and tangle with his beard. Both beard and locks were white, though the eyes which stared at the travelers from beneath bushy brows were not those of an old man.

"Who are you who come so boldly into the place of Regin?" asked the lord.

Sigurd made courteous answer, but he did so with the rightful pride of a king's son. "I am Sigurd, son of Sigmund, of the true line of the Volsungs. And I come in the service of Mimir Master-Smith, for the charcoal of your making."

"Ha, how can this be true speaking? I have not heard before that one of the Volsung blood serves a smith, be he master or less. Think up a better tale than that, my would-be hero!"

"There is no better tale than the truth," returned Sigurd, still with courtesy, though on his cheek was the flush of a man who has had his word doubted. "It was my father's will that, since I must someday rule, I should better know those whom I would rule. Therefore, I

44

should dwell among them for a space, working with my hands for my bread, even as they do."

Regin combed his beard with his fingers and nodded.

"A wise man, King Sigmund. And have you learned, Sigurd King's-Son, what it means to earn your bread with your two hands?"

"For a year have I done so, and Mimir Master-Smith has not yet turned me from his door as useless."

"Which is in your favor, King's-Son. Well enough, I accept your tale. Do you rest this night under my roof while those in my service make ready your charcoal."

He did not seem to notice Sig, and for that the boy was glad. He thought that he would not care to have this lord of the forest watch him too closely. Sig squatted in the shadows behind Sigurd, who sat in the guest chair. But his lord did not forget that he was there, for from time to time he tossed back a round of bread or a bone still heavy with meat, so that Sig ate as well as the high ones.

Regin suddenly leaned forward and asked, "Do you travel with a hound, King's-Son? One you must feed with the best from the table?"

"No hound, Lord Regin, but one who has been a good trail comrade to me, though he is young."

"Summon him forth that I may look upon him," commanded Regin.

There was no escape. Sig came out of the shadows to stand before Regin. Though he and Sigurd had washed well in a forest pool, and he had arranged his poor clothing as best he could, yet still he well knew that he was as a poor beggar. But he was also for the present a shield man to a king's son, and so he held himself stiff and straight.

"A comrade say you, Sigurd King's-Son? Ha! An ill choice! This is a plucked crow, a starveling, such as any snug-housed man can find whining for bread outside his door."

But Sigurd King's Son came down from the guest seat. As he made answer he laid his hand on Sig's shoulder. "This is one I would trust at my back in an hour of need. What man can ask more than that, Lord Regin?"

"It would seem that the whelp has more in him than readily meets the eye. Well enough, keep your hero, King's-Son." Regin laughed in such a way as made Sig feel hot and clench his good fist. Yet Sigurd's hand still rested on his shoulder and then drew him forward, so that he no longer lurked in the shadows but sat on the step of the guest chair in full sight of all, with his lord's favor plain.

Venison they ate, and wild honey, and white bread such as Sig had never seen, and grapes both tart and sweet on the tongue. Afterward they were led into a small side chamber for sleeping where there was a couch of myrtle and hemlock woven together cunningly to form a soft bed. Sig settled at the foot, wrapped in his cloak, but Sigurd stretched out full upon the boughs and slept.

When they awoke it was after sunup and Sigurd sat up with a strange look on his face.

"This night I did dream," he said in a low voice as if he spoke more to himself than to Sig. "And it was a dream of power, though I have not the wit to read it."

They went into the great hall and there Regin sat once more in the high seat, as if he had never moved through the long night past. Across his knees lay the harp of a bard. Now and then he absently plucked a string to bring forth a singing note. Before the guest seat there were bread, goat cheese, honey, and horns of barley beer. Regin waved them to sit and eat, and Sig again took his place on the seat's step.

"You slept well through the night?" Regin asked as might any ordinary host.

"I dreamed," Sigurd answered.

"And of what did you dream, King's-Son?"

"That I stood on a mountain peak, among other peaks, though none higher. And about me flew eagles, while snow lay at my feet. There were the Norns there—Urd, the Past, was to the east where the sun rises, and between her fingers she spun thread which glittered as if it were formed of that very sun.

"And Verdanda, the Present, was afar in the sea where sky and water meet. She caught up that thread and wove a web of purple and gold, richer than any king's wear I have seen. But even as she wove it, Skald, the dire Future, caught it from her and tore it to shreds, which she cast from her so that they fell at the cold white feet of yet another who watched. And she was Hel, who is queen over the dead. It seems to me that this was a dream which began well but ended ill."

"In this life many things begin well and end ill," Regin said. "Listen to one such—" And Regin, old as he was, lifted up his voice and sang.

His voice was full and strong, and that of a great bard. They listened as if caught in a witch wife's spell. Also, as he sang, he changed so that his white hair and beard faded away, and they saw not Regin the forest lord in that high seat but rather Mimir Master-Smith.

Then he put down the harp and laughed.

"Ay, I am Mimir, who was Regin. But that is another tale and the time had not yet come for the telling of it. But it is true that you have great deeds to do, Sigurd King's-Son. A sword you have, though it was forged from the shards of another, which was the All Father's gift—but not a kind one—to your forefather. Now you must

47

gain a horse such as will serve you as well as steel, perhaps even better."

"And where do I find such a horse, master?"

"You go to the north, to the giant Griph, and there ask it of him. On his pastures run the finest steeds in the world."

"Well enough." Sigurd nodded, "And this I am to do now?"

"What time is better?"

As Sigurd King's-Son prepared to go he shook his head at Sig, who stood waiting, with no sword at his belt but only the stoutest staff he could find in his hand.

"This is no quest for you, youngling."

"Lord, I do not stay behind. If you will not suffer me to go with you, then still shall I follow."

Sigurd looked at him for a long, long moment. Then he nodded again. "Well enough," he said as he had to Mimir-Regin. "It is in my mind that we are in some manner bound to the same fate, though why is not clear."

The way was long and they found night and day, night and day passing by. Sometimes they went through forests, or over bleak moorlands, or took steep mountain trails. They came to fine, fair lands and were feasted in halls and besought by lords to stay awhile, but Sigurd would not.

This road was not easy and Sig found it very hard indeed. No longer might he hide away his clawhand, for he needed it to hold onto rocks and bushes in places where the going was rough. He used it so much that he sometimes forgot how ill it looked.

At length they came to a place of snow where there was a hall built of huge boulders no human could have moved. White were its walls and within were green pillars which were very cold to the touch, as if they were carved of ice. There was a high seat made of the mighty teeth of seahorses, and over it hung a canopy of stone. He who sat there held a carved staff of ivory and wore a purple mantle, while his white beard hung nearly to the green floor.

He was large, so that to him Sigurd was as a small boy. But he smiled and made them welcome. And they sat down and broke their fast while he and Sigurd talked of the Midworld from which they had come, of the sky reaching above them, and of the seas framing the earth. And Sig, rested and well fed, listened. Nor was he aware of how long that fine, mind-filling talk lasted.

But at last Griph struck the tabletop with the point of his staff and spoke out. "Enough, Sigurd King's-Son. It is music to my ears, your voice, for it has been long since mortal man has sought me out with news of Midworld and what chances there. But it is to my mind that you have come for a reason, and that reason runs on four feet in my pastures. Is that not so?"

"Lord Griph, it is so."

"Thus be it. Go forth to my pastures, King's-Son, and choose wisely, for upon this may hang your life some day."

So they went out to the pastures. And there were such horses as Sig had never seen. Each one was finer than the finest in any king's stable in Midworld. He wondered how Sigurd could choose. But, even as he thought thus, a shadow fell across the stone where they stood. And there was a man.

Gray were his cloak and kirtle, blue his hood, and he wore a patch over one eye. But the other saw twice as keenly as any mortal, Sig believed.

"So, Sigurd Volsung, you have come to find a horse to match the sword you wear?"

"Ay, Great One."

"Then listen. Such choosing takes care. Drive this herd

to the river. The one that takes to the flood and swims over, then returns to you—he is Greykell and none other can equal him."

"My thanks to you, Great One."

But he of the one eye did not smile. "Give thanks later, Sigurd, when the thread is all spun, the web full woven, and Skald has finished her part in the matter. That time is yet afar, but it still lies before you."

Sigurd bowed his head a little. "What man can change the will of Skald? I shall do what must be done to the best of my doing."

"Which is all any man can say. Go you now and take Greykell."

Once more he was gone as if he had never stood there. But Sig was wiser now than he had been at the forge. This was surely Odin All-Father come to take a part in their fate, and so he was also more than a little frightened.

It went even as the stranger had said. Sig and Sigurd drove the horses to the river bank. All refused the flood except one, and he swam across and on the far shore reared and trumpeted a challenge. Then he returned and came to Sigurd, nuzzling at the hands held out to him.

Strong was Greykell, strong enough to carry them both back on the long journey to Regin's hall in the forest. Once more they feasted, and when they were done with food and drink Regin-Mimir took up his harp. This time he sang a tale which cast a heavy spell, for it was fashioned out of his own memories—a strange, dark story.

It began in the older days, when the Asakind had walked more often in the Midworld clothed with men's bodies. So came Odin All-Father, giving men knowledge and strength, and with him Holnir, who brought cheer and laughter. Yet with them skulked Loki in a dark cloud of cunning, deceit, and base thoughts.

During such a far-faring, Loki, for wicked sport, slew Oddar, who had taken on the seeming of an otter that he might explore the depths of a lake. And then he gave the otter's body to Oddar's father, Hreidmar, as a dreadful jest. Then had Hreidmar called upon his other sons, Fafnir and Regin, and together they demanded blood ransom in gold, enough to cover the otter's hide.

The Asakind cast lots, and Loki was so selected to go for the gold, Odin and Holnir standing hostage. Loki bargained with the sea queen Ran for her fine net, and with this in hand he caught fast the dwarf king Andvari, who had hidden in the scaled skin of a salmon. From Andvari, in return for his freedom, Loki took the great treasure of the dwarfs. He also tore from Andvari's own finger a ring in the form of a snake, its tail gripped by its fangs. Diamonds were the scales of that snake, rubies its eyes.

Then Andvari cast a mighty spell to curse the treasure and the ring. But Loki laughed as he bore it away to the hall of Hreidmar. There they spread out the otter skin, and it became larger and larger, until it covered most of the floor. On it Loki heaped and leveled the treasure. Yet, when he had done, there was still a single hair left uncovered, so he must also cast down upon that the ring, and so with it he cast the curse.

The Asakind, the blood debt paid, went their way. But Hreidmar, looking upon the vast treasure, lusted for it. And when he touched the ring, behold, he became himself just such a serpent as it was in form. Regin cried out at this sight and fled. But his brother Fafnir drew sword and killed the serpent, once his father.

Then, in turn, he looked upon the gold, and he, too, lusted for it so greatly that it became all the world to him. He bore it off to a far wasteland and there he spread it out to feast his eyes upon it. Among all else was a fine helm of gold made like a dragon's head. Fafnir put this on, and as the ring had made his sire a serpent, so did the helm make of him a dragon.

Thus through the years the treasure lay in the waste guarded by the dragon, Fafnir, who had forgotten he had ever been a man. Not until he was slain would evil depart from the land. Many had been the men who had tried to reach the treasure, only to die. Now Sigurd had been chosen by fate to end the rule of Fafnir.

Sigurd King's-Son listened and, when Regin sang no more, he spoke. "So be it, Regin who was Mimir, who was once host to the Asakind. I shall deal with your dragon brother."

"But not alone!" Regin was no longer like Mimir now, but different once again, being gray and wrinkled of skin as if many years of time had passed. His eyes were not those of mortal man, so that Sig dreaded them and was glad they were not turned in his direction. "I shall ride with you."

"And I," Sig said, for he knew that he must. Perhaps Regin did not like that, for he shot a single disturbing glance at Sig. But he did not dispute Sig's words openly.

Seven days they went, until they came to a land broken by great chasms. There were many tall black boulders, but nothing grew among them. This way lay twisted at the foot of a mountain up which they must climb and climb, even though their breath came in gasps and their strength failed. Sigurd, who was the strongest, ever led the way.

On the other side of the mountain was a plain, which they looked down upon at nightfall. Around circles of flickering flames moved a vast, dark shape which Sig, for one, wanted to see no closer. They descended to the bank of a river which lay between them and the plain. The water was thick and dark as if it were not water at all, but an evil slime. And there were stirrings in it as if hidden, nameless monsters moved below its surface.

Though it was day by the time they reached the bank of that dark and threatening stream, no sun warmed the sky. Nor could they see any clouds, but only a gray light hardly clearer than night dusk. Through that shone the glow of the cursed treasure. Yet there was that about it which also beckoned one, made a man wish to seize it piece upon piece.

Gems lay there, set in crowns of kings long forgotten, bracelets and necklets, and rings, jewel-hilted swords, blazoned shields, all tumbled together in heaps. And from one to another of these crawled the guardian on his ceaseless rounds.

The dull light, and also a kind of mist which arose from the treasure, were such that one could not clearly see Fafnir. That he had ever existed in the form of a man Sig found hard to believe. This creature was as great as the giant Griph, yet it crawled upon its belly, holding a horned head but a little above the ground. A long tail dragged behind it and the stumps of small wings were on its shoulders.

They could see on the further bank a smoothed rut in the clay leading down to the water's edge. Perhaps that marked Fafnir's path to drink.

"Would you swim?" Regin-Mimir squatted on the bank, gazing down into the water. Now he took his staff and this he pushed into the flood as if testing for a ford. There was a flurry and a swirling of water. He gave a cry and jerked back. But what he held now was only half a staff. The rest was gone, as if sheared off by giant jaws.

"It would seem," Sigurd said, looking at this grim proof of what lay beneath the surface, "that swimming is not the answer."

Regin-Mimir glanced at him slyly, and Sig liked less

and less what he guessed might lie at the back of those eyes which were no longer a man's eyes.

"How then, do you, reach that which you have come to slay?"

Even as he spoke there came a boat on the river. From whence it came, and why they had not sighted it before, Sig did not know. It was like one of the small craft used on lakes by fall-time hunters of wild fowl, and a single man sat in it, making easy play with the oars. Sig half expected each time the oars dipped into the water to see them rise again splintered and riven, yet they remained whole and unscarred.

The man who used them wore a hood of blue, though his head was bent so that in this half light they could not see his face. But Sig did not doubt that there was a patch over one eye on that face. And he shivered a little, took a tighter grip upon his staff.

"Hail, Sigurd Volsung!" The stranger brought the boat to the bank and stepped out of it to face them. Though he did not tie the craft, yet it did not drift with the current but remained fast.

"Hail, All Father!" This time Sigurd dared give name to the other. "Being who you are, you know the reason for our coming."

The one eye seemed to rest not only on Sigurd but on his companions also. And Sig could not look away. What could they do save as the Norns decided when Odin All-Father himself took a hand in their future?

"The reason is known," said the stranger. "No man, no, or Asakind can turn or alter the weaving of fate and fortune. Since the beginning of this venture was partly of my doing, so now I must aid in the ending. No mortal man or Asakind can meet Fafnir in open battle. So thus you must do: Once a day, close to eventide, Fafnir comes to drink at the river—you can see the path he has worn over there across the water. Do you dig a pit there, and put on it a light covering of earth, hiding yourself thereunder. Then when Fafnir passes above you, stab upward into his softer lower parts, which is the only place even Balmung can find entrance."

"For your aid, All Father, are we grateful."

The stranger shook his head slowly. "For that thanks wait until your life's ending, Sigurd King's-Son. For good does not always give birth to good. Sometimes evil comes instead. However, this is your fate and so it must be. And the plan is the best I can give you."

He turned then and took a step or two from them and was gone. But Regin-Mimir scuttled forward and laid hand upon the boat, looking over his shoulder to say eagerly, "There is but little time to make the trap. Let us go, Sigurd King's-Son, soon to be Sigurd Fafnir's-Bane."

So they passed across the river, Sigurd taking one oar, Sig the other. Regin-Mimir played no part in that rowing, looking ever to the other bank as if by his eagerness alone he could hasten their progress. They found the track of the dragon and it was as deep as Sigurd was tall; also its walls were encrusted with slime that gave off an evil smell to sicken a man. Nor were there any lack of warnings of what had happened to those who dared enter Fafnir's land. A skull rolled from Sig's foot as he took an unwary step. And there lay a sword, its blade half melted away.

Sigurd leaped down into the center of that noisome way and with Balmung he hacked at the earth packed down by the dragon's foul weight. The slimed soil he so loosened he passed up to Sig, who bore it away in a bag made of his cloak to dump in another place. Again Regin-Mimir took no part in their labors. Rather, he sat hunched together like a great gray spider, staring out to that plain where the treasure fires burned and Fafnir crawled to make sure not a single piece had been taken away.

At last they were done, for Sigurd could fit himself into the pit he had hacked out. Then Sig dropped down and spread out his befouled cloak over Sigurd, over its surface sprinkling the disturbed earth, until he hoped that it looked as it had before their coming. Then he climbed out once more and went to Regin-Mimir, touching him on the arm. The Master Smith seemed to awaken from a dream, for he arose stiffly to go to the boat. This time he, too, lent his strength to an oar, and they rowed back to where they had left Greykell and their other horses. Those stood with bent heads from their great weariness.

Now there was only the waiting, and Sig found that the worst of all. At last the dusk, which here was day, became darker so that the treasure fires burned brighter. As Fafnir's monstrous shadow turned from them to the river path, Sig gripped his staff so hard that his nails bit into its wood and his hands ached. To see that great scaled thing slip along the rut its body had worn in the earth was a fearsome sight. And Sig knew then that he was of no hero blood to lie now as Sigurd lay, enduring until the time came for attack.

The dragon's body slipped on, and now the horned head was very close to the river. Had Sigurd been smothered, crushed by its passing? Surely he would have struck before this—!

But even as Sig's fear swelled, the forepart of the dragon reared high, and from its throat came such a sound as made the very ground about them tremble. Its tail lashed and beat upon the earth, driving deep into the surface any rock it chanced to strike. From a gaping hole in the belly poured a dark stream of foul liquid. Writhing, Fafnir reached the river, and now his head went down and he bit at his own wound as if to punish it for the hurt it caused him.

Twisting, turning, the dragon fought death, until his great body reared once too often and he toppled into the water, where wings, great-nailed limbs, dangerous tail, beat the dark liquid into a stinking froth. Around him all the water was troubled, as those who lived within its depths gathered for such a feasting as they had never expected. So a second battle raged. Sig found he could not watch, but hid his face in his hands, and tried not to listen either.

By some good fortune the struggle in the river did not wreck or bear away their boat. When Sig dared to look, and there was no more disturbance in the water, he ran to the craft and readied oars.

"Master!" He called to Regin-Mimir, who sat still upon a rock gazing at the river with a strange smile on his lips. "Master, we must go to Lord Sigurd!"

"Ay." The Master Smith arose and came to take up one of the oars. And he pulled with a will to match Sig's, as they sent the boat over water.

Hardly had they touched the shore so torn by the dragon's last struggles than Sig leaped up it and ran to Fafnir's path. For Sigurd had not come forth from that hiding place and the boy feared that the worst must have happened—that in slaying he had also been slain.

The trenchway was half full of the dark liquid which had gushed from Fafnir's body, and from it a great stench arose. Sig prepared to plunge into it, poisonous though it was. However, as he reached the place where he thought the pit must be, there was movement. And out of that stinking flow arose he whom they sought, but so bedaubed and encrusted he did not seem a man. And he staggered and wavered as if wounded.

Somehow Sig drew his lord forth and wrenched off his

own kirtle for want of a better cleanser to wipe the slime from Sigurd, who was gasping as if he could not draw enough air into his laboring lungs.

"Lord, where are your hurts?" Sig worked frantically to clean away the muck and see how badly the other had suffered.

But already Sigurd stood straighter and breathed more freely. "No hurts," he panted. "It was but the stench of the beast and that which flowed from it. Balmung did well its work. Fafnir is dead, the treasure freed."

Again and again he thrust the great sword deep into the ground to clean its blade. Then with Sig he turned to look over the plain where lay the piles of riches. Though the dark of night was full upon them, the fires lit by the dragon's hoard allowed them to see not only what lay there but the stark land itself.

And running from one heap to the next was a small, shrunken figure. Here it plucked a crown and held it high, only to let it clatter back again. There it swung a glittering necklace as a slinger swings his weapon before he hurls the stone. Again it kicked at a shield and sent it clanging. Then it flung forth its arms as if to gather to its shrunken chest all that lay there, to hold it so forever.

Regin-Mimir! But where was the wise Master Smith whom Sig had known for most of his short life? This—this creature was not him. Regin-Mimir was changed, perhaps not into a dragon, but—

Suddenly the figure capering among the piles of treasure turned to face them. And Sig saw lips pull tight against teeth in a grin which was not that of a man. The figure swooped upon a pile of glitter and came up with a flashing thing in one hand. Then it ran toward them with a speed greater than Greykell's gallop.

"Mine! Mine!" Regin-Mimir screeched as he came. "Mine the treasure. Death to those who would take it!"

He took no measures for defense but, wild of eye, rushed at Sigurd. Sig saw that what he held was a long-bladed dagger, very bright and keen of edge. But Balmung arose and Sigurd struck.

The stooped and withered body, which had drawn age more and more about it as a cloak during these past hours, fell. Yet still the head strained upward from the hunched shoulders, and out of that twisted mouth came one last word, flung as a challenge: "Mine!"

Sig shrank back. Sigurd unfastened his stained and bedraggled cloak and stooped to throw it over the huddled form.

"He was a master smith and once a man of honor," he said in a low voice. "He could not slay his dragon, but was slain thereby."

"His dragon?"

"Ay. Greed was his dragon, and it bides here still. So Fafnir shall guard, though he be dead. The treasure is rightly cursed. Let who dares lift it. But it is better to leave it here until the end of the world."

And Sig, watching those pale, ghostly lights burning here like damning fires, knew this to be the truth.

So in the end they rode forth from the waste, leaving it all behind them. On they went to fulfill the weaving of the Norns, living the lives allotted to them.

3

SIRRUSH-LAU

"Let it lie as Sigurd Fafnir's-Bane said, let it lie—"

The words echoed around in the dusty, gloomy room. Sig raised his head. His hands were before him, gripping the table edge so hard they ached. He should have been holding a staff—and where was the river—the mountains —Greykell and the other horses? He shook his head, trying to throw off the remnants of that dream. Or had it been a dream? So real—so very real! You did not eat in dreams, or get tired, or *feel*. Sigurd had been real, and Mimir, and Fafnir—

There was Fafnir still before him, silver-bright. Sig raised his hand to sweep away the pieces of the puzzle he had so painstakingly put together—the silver dragon. But somehow he could not touch it. It would be—it would feel—NO!

He pushed back the chair so hastily it fell with a bang to the floor. Outside there was a flash of lightning and he knew where he was, though he was not yet sure just what had happened to him. He only knew that he wanted to get away—go home—

Sig ran, out of the room, back to the old kitchen. The rain was beating in through the open window. But he remembered there was something else—the table—Ras—

He hesitated as he reached the window. Least of all did he want another fight now. But he did not, could not, leave Ras shut in the basement. Sig dashed for the table against the door, gave it furious jerks with all the strength he could muster, pulling it farther away from the door. Then he waited no longer, making for the window, and the rain and dark beyond.

The overgrown bushes of the unkempt garden caught at him as he plunged on, by the shortest way, to that outer world he could believe in. But the other world was a part of him still. He could see in his mind the forge with Sigurd King's-Son beating out the mighty sword, the forest hall of Mimir-Regin, the long journey to reach the terrible, blasted land of Fafnir.

Treasure! That word, which had always been so exciting, meant something different now. Fafnir had taken the treasure and turned from man into monster because of his greed for it. Mimir, who had been Sigurd's master and good friend—when the treasure had lain before him, he, too, became a monster, in another way. Then Sigurd had made his choice, to leave the evil, and so he had gone away a hero.

Sig went over and over those memories as he ran for home. It must be awfully late. Dad would be there, he would want to know where Sig had been. But if he told, no one would believe him! Just as he could not make up any story, either. Sig Clawhand could not have lied his way out of trouble. If Dad did ask any questions he would have to tell the part about going into the old house, finding the puzzle. But telling the rest—that he could not!

There was no one home. When he came in the kitchen door he glanced up at the clock on the shelf, stared at it in disbelief, and then went over to shake it. Five o'clock—only half an hour—he had only been away half an hour!

Still finding that hard to believe, Sig shrugged out of his wet raincoat. He had beat Dad home after all, and he would not have to tell. But still tugging at his mind was the thought of Ras.

He had heard nothing from the basement when he

pulled aside the table he had used to bar the door. What if in the dark down there Ras had fallen, or been hurt? No one knew he was there, no one but Sig. It would be Sig's fault if Ras was lying now at the foot of the steps in the dark, maybe with a broken leg, no one knowing—

Slowly Sig looked at the clock again, being prodded into doing what he least wanted: going back to the house, making sure that Ras was all right. Dad would come for sure if he left now, then Sig would have to explain everything.

Ras was tough, he was probably already out of the basement and on the way home. But if he were not? Sig buttoned up his slicker. He picked up the note his mother had left, took out his ballpoint, and added a line. At least Dad would know that he had been home and would be back.

Not daring to stop, bcause if he did he might not be able to make himself go back through the rain and the dark to the house, Sig started out.

Ras sat in the dark. He had explored with his hands earlier, knew that he was on a stairway. What lay below he did not want to know. He had yelled, that was while he was still angry. Then his anger had gone, as if the cold from below had frozen it out of him, and he was only afraid. After that he had called and pounded on the door. But everything was so quiet that he knew Sig must have walked right out of the house and left him!

What was it about the box that had upset Sig so? Funny how Ras had been able to find it so easily, just as if Sig had left a sign pointing to it, the way his tracks had shown up so plainly in the floor dust and that sheet had been left pulled crooked with the box just shoved under it.

Nothing in the box to be excited about—a jigsaw puzzle. Ras had expected to find something really worth-while after Sig's talk about hidden treasure. Ras tried to push aside fear by considering something else. Think logically, Shaka always said. He sure wished he had told Shaka about this last night. Only, his brother had been out to a meeting. And when he came home he and Dad had had a big row. Mom had cried. It had been a mess. Lots of things were a mess nowadays, with Shaka talking one thing, Dad another.

No one knew he was here, no one was going to come looking for him. He was on his own and he would have to get out by himself. Ras went back up to the stubborn door, laid the palms of his hands flat against it and shoved, though that did not seem to do any good. But he did not give up trying, and that little crack of light now showing around the edge was better than the dark in the other direction.

Then he heard the pound of feet running across the old floor boards. He had been listening so hard for that. Sig—Sig was coming back, and in a big hurry, from the front of the house. What had he been doing all this time? It seemed to Ras in the dark that he had been here hours at least.

He pushed against the door. Sig had to let him out! He couldn't go away and leave Ras penned up in here, or could he? Just the sort of trick a whitey would play. Shaka said never to trust—Ras opened his mouth to yell. But those steps were coming toward the door now. Don't let Sig know he was ready to call for help—never let him know that! Say nothing, just jump him when he got the door open.

Ras heard the grate of the table on the floor, waited for Sig to open the door. But instead there was a sound, quickly lost in a clap of thunder, of feet moving off. Ras threw himself at the door. It opened farther than it had before, then banged against the table again, but now there was a crack large enough for Ras to squeeze through. A moment later he was in the kitchen.

What had Sig been doing all this time in the house? The window was still propped open, rain coming in. It was late, Ras knew he had better be getting home. Still his curiosity held him, he had to know what had kept Sig there. He had a flashlight of his own, smaller than Sig's, but it would give him light enough. That box of jigsaw pieces, why was it so important? Had Sig spent all this time finding another hiding place for it?

Ras went into the front room. No covers were pulled off the furniture. Most everything looked as if it had not been touched for a long time. He went on down the hall to the doorway of that other room. There his flashlight beam picked up the chair, now lying on its side. And the tabletop was a glitter of color.

He crossed the room quickly to shine his light directly down on the table. Queer how bright it looked. But there were only pieces of a jigsaw, part of them put together to make a silver dragon. Was *that* what Sig had been doing here? Why in the world would he sit in this dark room and put together part of an old puzzle, shutting Ras up while he worked on it, as if it were some big secret?

Odd looking—Ras had seen a lot of puzzles, but none so bright as this one. And that dragon, when you looked right at him he seemed to move. Only, you could not be sure you saw him do that, you only felt so.

This was the puzzle Sig had fought him for. Yet he had gone now and left it lying here. Ras put out his hand, intending to sweep it all into the waiting box. It would serve Sig right if he took it home with him.

Only, he discovered that he could not touch those pieces, move them. Abruptly he turned and went out of the room. Let it stay right there, then. Who wanted that old puzzle, anyway? It wasn't worth anything.

Ras hurried through the house and climbed out of the window. He was halfway down the drive when he saw Sig pass under the street light on his way back. Ras pushed into the bushes. Was he coming back for his precious puzzle?

As Sig went straight to the window and crawled through, Ras dodged along behind, watching. He was up on the porch as soon as Sig was inside. Now he could see the other's flashlight beam illuminating the basement door. Sig had laid the light on top of the table as he tugged and pulled at it. Then he disappeared through the basement door. He must have gone a ways down the stair. But he was not going to find what he hunted for.

Ras ran for home. Let whitey stay there and hunt—do him good. But why had Sig come back—to fight again? Ras was puzzled.

Luck was with him, he was able to get in and up to his room without being seen. Shaka's voice, and Mom's, came from the front of the house. Mom sounded upset, as she was a lot lately when Shaka talked about what his protest crowd planned. Ever since Shaka had dropped out of college Mom had taken it hard. Just as she took it hard when Shaka stopped going to church and spoke mean about what the preacher was trying to do with the Head Start classes.

Ras sat down on the edge of the bed and looked at the posters Shaka had given him for the wall. One had a big black fist raised against a red background and a lot of foreign words printed under it. Shaka said that was Swahili, their own language, and they ought to learn how to speak it. It was being taught now in the Afro-studies school Shaka had helped to start.

But Ras hardly saw that familiar black and red now,

just as the voices from below were a meaningless mur-mur. What he continued to think about was the puzzle laid out on the table, that silver dragon which had seemed to move when you were not looking at it square-ly, but was firmly fixed when you did.

There had been four dragons pictured on the lid of the box, he now remembered. A red one, a yellow one, and a blue. The blue one—once he had thought of it Ras could not get it out of his mind. Yet he had no clear mental pic-ture of it at all—just the bright blue color.

Sig had gone down in the cellar on his return, to see where Ras was, he was sure of that. But would he also take away the puzzle? Suddenly Ras was uneasy. What was the matter? That puzzle, it was not important. But—he did not want Sig to take it! He, Ras, wanted to see it again!

Tomorrow was Friday, and after school Mom was going to pick him up and go and get some new shoes. There was no getting out of that. Saturday morning—it was going to be a long time until Saturday morning, that was for sure.

A loud banging of the door broke through his plans. Shaka was going out. He always banged that door when he was angry. Now Mom would be upset all evening, and Dad, when he came home, would be worse than Mom, because he got really sore at Shaka. Ras shook his head and stood up to put away his jacket. He wished there was not all this arguing, but the things Shaka said did make sense. Look at Dad, he worked hard all his life, never got better jobs—just because he was black. Nowa-days people did not have to take it, no, they did not. Yet here was Dad saying it was wrong to do anything against the law. Shaka said as long as there were two laws, one for whitey and one for the black man, then the black man had to do something about it.

69

"George?" That was Mom from the foot of the stairs.

"Yes, I'm here," he answered in a hurry. No use trying the "Ras" business on Mom or Dad.

"You have a half hour for homework before supper." She was always counting off time that way. And when Dad came home and upstairs to clean up for supper, he would look in to see what books Ras had brought home.

They wanted him to get on the honor list, go to college. But Shaka said— Ras moved the school books around on the desk Dad had fitted up for him. It sure was hard in the family nowadays. When he listened to Dad it made sense, and when he listened to Shaka it made sense, too—only what they said were two different things.

He shuffled through the pages in his notebook, not really looking for his assignment but thinking again about that puzzle and the silver dragon Sig had put together. Why had Sig started working it right there? You would think he would have taken it home.

Ras sighed. Too many questions, and he seldom found answers which seemed to suit anyone, even himself. He wondered what Sig would say or do when they met at the bus stop in the morning. If Sig tried to start anything —just let him look out! Ras had him to thank for that dark, cold wait on the basement stairs, and that was something he would not forget in a hurry.

Ras was so interested in what Sig would do that he managed to get to the bus stop earlier than usual the next morning. The Chinese kid, Kim Stevens, again was up against the wall, as if he needed something behind him. He had his book bag between his feet and was reading a paperback book. Always had his nose in a book, that one. And Artie Jones was holding a new football, smacking it back and forth between his hands. He was whistling, paying no attention to Kim. But Sig was not to be seen. Yes—here he came, almost running, his windbreaker unzipped, his cap so far back on his head it was almost falling off.

Sig stared straight at Ras, a queer expression on his face. And he slowed to a walk, then glanced quickly away. The bus was coming as Sig halted beside Artie and started talking in a fast gabble. They waded in through the crowd of little kids. Kim had his finger between the pages of his book to mark his place. He went on reading as soon as they sat down, as if Ras, sharing his seat, were invisible. Artie, across the aisle, was talking about the football. Ras had Artie sized up as a big talker. He ran after the Ross gang, not that they wanted him.

Ras slipped lower in his seat and thought. He had his plans made for Saturday. There were his regular house jobs, sure. One of those was to go down to the laundromat. He could set the clothes washing there and then beat it for awhile. The laundry was only two blocks over from the old house—and there he could see about the puzzle.

He did not know why he wanted to look at it, but somehow he knew that he had to. Though, of course, if Sig had already taken it he certainly would never see it again.

The next day it worked out smoothly enough. Ras got the laundry down and in the washer. He now had twenty-five minutes, and if he ran both ways he ought to have plenty of time to get to the house and back. As he hurried along he watched for Sig. Down the block Artie was kicking his football around. There was no one near the wall and Ras dodged in, making his way as quickly as possible behind the bushes.

He waited and watched for a long minute before he went up on the porch, struggled with the window, propping it up with the same brick Sig had used. Once inside he stood and listened. There were faint sounds from without, but quiet within.

With as little noise as possible, Ras crept through the rooms, down the hall to the room with the table. A bar of light coming through the open inner shutter fell squarely on the table and chair.

The puzzle was still there, Sig had not taken it. And it was exactly as Ras had seen it last, the silver dragon coiled and rearing in a way which made it look alive.

Somehow Ras found himself sitting down, studying the partly completed puzzle. He knew what he had to do—put together some more of it. He picked up the lid of the box, traced with his fingertip the bisecting lines which divided it into four parts—the silver dragon at the top, the red dragon to his left, the gold-yellow one to his right, and the queer blue one, very unlike the other three, far more stiff and strange looking, at the bottom. Then he was pushing out of the way the reds and the yellows, concentrating on gathering all the blue ones in a heap.

And he forgot, as he hurried over that sorting, time or where he was, or anything but the need to fit one piece to another, and the next to that, and to that. The blue dragon now had one leg, back haunches—now two hind-feet with their birdlike claws, a tail, long and thin, held up at a stiff angle to match the long, snaky neck at the other end. Now—here was part of a paw—why did the thing have paws like a lion in front and bird claws at the back? Yes, that was the other leg! No—rather a part of the neck. Ras paused to study the picture on the box more carefully.

The head had a curled bit like a mane, and a cone-shaped horn halfway down the creature's nose. He had the head nearly done. Some more bits of upper neck—

As he picked and chose, fitted and discarded, Ras knew a growing excitement. There was something about this strange picture that he knew, had seen before; only, he could not remember when or where. He frowned as he hunted for the section that would unite head with body. Suddenly he closed his eyes, trying to think of the whole thing as a picture and not a puzzle. Where had he seen it? Something Shaka had shown him? A picture in a book? Memory stirred very faintly.

All done now but one piece of clawed paw. Ras hesitated, trying again to remember how—when—where— This must be the right piece, but it was upside down. Those queer marks on the back looked like little wedges set in a broken pattern.

He remembered! Writing! He had seen that writing in a history book—Sumerian writing! Those wedges were made on clay with a stick and then baked so that the blocks of clay were books! Ras was surprised at the clearness with which it came back to his mind now. Carefully he detached two of the pieces he had fitted in earlier and turned them over. Each piece had some of the wedge writing, though each was different. The Sumerians had lived a very long time ago. What would their writing be doing here on the back of the puzzle?

It had something to do with the dragon, he was sure of that. Bricks! Yes, bricks! He suddenly saw the picture his mind had been seeking—a wall and on it this queer shape made of colored bricks.

"Sirrush-Lau!"

Ras started, looked around the many-shadowed room. Who had said that? He—he must have! But how—why?

Sirrush-Lau. He stared down at the creature now complete. That was its name. And it blazed up at him fiercely as if brilliantly lighted by a hot sun.

PRINCE SHERKARER

The sun blazed, so strongly that the brick pavement of the wharf was oven-hot. Yet inside himself Sherkarer shivered with cold. But to let these pale-faced barbarians know that he had ever been touched by fear—! He stared straight ahead, his head as proudly high as he could hold it: he, who was of the blood of Nubian Piankhay, Lord of the Two Lands, Pharaoh of Egypt, a slave in this place of towering walls and strange, bearded men.

He need only glance at his own wrist to see the blue tattoo marks braceleting his dark brown arm—the coiled Serpent with the lion head of the great god Apedemek—to remember how it had been. How long ago? One day wove into the next and the next. First only a blurred misery of pain, which had fogged his mind after the war ax had smashed against his skull at the taking of Napata, City of Kings. Later, when his wits had returned to him, he had found himself a war captive, sold as a slave. Ah, that was a drinking of bitterness!

There is no medicine to cure hatred, and he hated hotly those who had taken but not killed him at Napata, as well as the trader who had bought him, and those jostling around him now. He might not yet wear the lion-claw scars of a warrior across his cheeks, but he had fought in the defense, his bow well drawn until the arrows failed and the Egyptian forces broke in, those Egyptians who hated all the men of Nubia since the days Piankhay had shown them to be only shadow men in battle and had taken their throne.

The Nubians had held that throne, too, until generations later, Pharaoh Tanwetamani had at last been driven south once more, but not by Egyptians! No, it had taken the Assyrian war host to do that. This time, along with the Egyptians who had stormed Napata were mainly barbarians, white-skinned sea rovers, clanless men who had taken service in the north.

Not that they had found the men of Napata, or Meroë, easy meat. Sherkarer's lips flattened against his teeth in a silent snarl. Ay, they had paid a full price for the sacking of the city. Though to remember that did not ease his heart now, since he was not among those who had managed to retreat farther south to Meroë.

He had no bow, no sword hung in a shoulder sling ready for his drawing, no ax to hand. He was as those men on the wharf stripped to breechclouts, working to haul up the largest piece of cargo in the ship which had come up river at early dawn. That cargo—Sherkarer shivered.

He knew the wild hunters of the marshes south of Meroë. Had he not, from the time he stood upon his two feet and ran about his mother's courtyards, heard the strange tales they could spin? For his mother was Bartare, Princess of Meroë, grand-daughter to the Candace, the Queen-Mother. At her court gathered all those who came and went into far lands, that she might hear what they had to tell and report it to Napata.

In those days, merchants from the caravans to the gulf ports, men out of the south where there were many strange and almost unbelievable things, told their stories and the scribes wrote them down. So the marsh hunters had talked of the lau—the demon-monster of the swamplands—until at last the Candace had decreed that this thing be captured and brought to her that she might make an offering of it to Apedemek. And Pharaoh Asopleta, her Son by the Favor of Amun, gave his seal to that order.

When the Great Voice speaks, men obey. It had taken

a full year and twenty days more. Men died in ways the survivors would not speak of save in whispers, looking over their shoulders to the right and left as they did so. Finally the lau was brought caged to Meroë. Those who saw it knew that it could only be a demon, for no normal beast would have had such an appearance. Yet it had been netted by men, put in a cage, carried north. So who could doubt the courage of any man out of Nubia?

Sherkarer, looking now upon that cage set on rollers, that curtained cage, wondered what those about him would think if the matting screen about it should suddenly fall and they could see what manner of creature they transported. He wished that would happen, for he was sure he would see all this company flee.

He thought again of the past, the days at court, before his enslavement. He remembered well how the lau had been sent from Meroë to the palace of the Candace at Napata. And Sherkarer had gone with the party guarding it. His mother had wished to bring him so to the attention of the Great Lady, thus to take the first step along the road of her future favor. He had pleased the Candace, though the lau had not. For she straightway ordered it covered again after she looked upon it, taken away to the temple of Apedemek. But the priests there had not slain it, but carefully tended it, planning to make its sacrifice the center of the great midyear ceremonies. Only, before that time had arrived, the Egyptians and the barbarian mercenaries had struck.

After the taking of Napata, which he could not remember to the end, Sherkarer had found himself part of the booty along with the lau. Why the monster had been preserved, he did not know. It was a thing of ill omen. Look how Napata had fared after it was brought to that city, and how those who had borne it north had suffered.

Sherkarer was captive; the rest, he thought, were all dead. Again Sherkarer snarled.

But the lau and the Sherkarer had been bought by the merchant Cha-paz and now they were both in this city of white-skinned, crocodile-souled barbarians. Had the lion-god Apedemek disliked the monster so much that he arranged this defeat for his own people so that it might be gone from his temple?

If so, was Sherkarer cursed because he had helped to take the monster to Napata? Yet he had only acted under orders, and those the orders of the Great One, Daughter of Apedemek, Lioness of the Land.

His lips moved now, though he did not speak aloud, in that prayer he had heard each morning at sunrise:

"Thou are greeted, Apedemek, Lord of Napata
Splendid God, at the head of Nubia.
Lion of the South, strong of arm.
Great God, who comes to him and calls.
Who is a companion for men and women,
Who will not be hindered in heaven nor earth."

"You, black one, down!"

That ever-ready lash curled about Sherkarer's shoulders, shocking him into awareness of what was going on about him. The slaves who had been dragging the curtained lau cage were lying face down on the wharf. Other men, free-born, had fallen to their knees, their arms crossed over their breasts, their heads bowed. There was the sound of horns. A procession was coming.

The lash licked painfully at Sherkarer's shoulders.

"Down, slave. You do not look upon the Great King's Chamberlain!"

Sherkarer knelt. It was that or be beaten senseless, as

he had discovered the first time his captors had had their will of him.

There was a saying of the peasants—the rat cannot call the cat to account. But it was also true that if the moon moves but slowly, still it crosses the city. Who holds the whip today may not curl his fingers about its butt tomorrow.

Kneel he would, but they could not force him to measure his body on the bricks with those laboring slaves. And perhaps they dared not extract full punishment for his stubbornness in the presence of the lord who came, for he did not feel the whip again.

The Nubian had learned enough of his owner's tongue during the long trip from Napata to understand most of what was said to him. But the rush of chanted words he heard now was a meaningless gabble. First came a guard of soldiers, walking stiffly in their overlapping scale armor, their curled beards forming a second breastplate across their chests.

Then followed a chariot with a driver and a passenger, and youthful men in rich dress flanking it on foot. Sherkarer peered sideways to see, though his head was bowed. There were two plumed fans held behind the man who rode in the chariot.

But he was no fine figure of a warrior. Rather, he was small and fat, so that his bloated stomach was thrust out before him to make a mound of his rich robe. His beard had been carefully curled and shone with oil, as did the long ringlets which fell to touch his shoulders, held in order by a broad gold band. His robe was yellow, the shawl-like cloak over it red, fastened upon one shoulder with a brooch which flashed gem-fire.

"A hundred lives to the favored of the King!" Sherkarer was now able to understand that. "May Ashpezaa, Favored of Mardek, live long!"

The guardsmen spread out in a line as the chariot came to a halt, and the young men who had walked on foot beside it gathered in a close knot. Ashpezaa, the Chamberlain, made no move, but his driver raised a whip to beckon imperiously.

The merchant Cha-paz hunkered forward on his knees, not rising to his feet. The courtiers made way for him as he so crawled to one side of the chariot, where the driver gave some order.

Cha-paz backed away in the same awkward fashion, to make a gesture of his own to the man who was overseeing the slave laborers. On his hands and knees the overseer went to the side of the covered cage and loosed the ties of the matting screen, his efforts matched by those of the second-in-command on the other side of the shrouded box.

The matting creaked, wrinkled in pleats, as they drew it aside. There was a strong whiff of the evil odor of the lau, and a strange noise as daylight reached into the cage, for the lau was a night creature and resented both light and heat.

That shadowy form moved, rattled the cage, as a horn-nosed head struck against the thrice-reinforced bars. Cries of alarm arose from the slaves, startled from their abject abasement before the official. And the guards swung up their stabbing spears at the ready, as if they feared the monster would break free.

Even the lord shifted his position as he stared at what he could see of the captive. Then, at a second sign from the driver, the matting fell back into place and was knotted down. Cha-paz once again was summoned closer.

This time Ashpezaa spoke, though he did not turn his head to look at the man waiting so humbly. Then the merchant squirmed away in a hurry, saving himself from

79

being trampled on as the chariot, guards, and followers started off.

Those withdrew toward the city, for this was the wharf which served the temple. That much Sherkarer already knew. In this land the temple had its own merchants to buy and sell afar, and its buildings sprawled as wide as any Nubian town of good size.

Now the whips of the overseers cracked once more and the cage on its rollers began to edge on at a very slow pace. Sherkarer got to his feet. Between his ankles was a bar of bronze to keep him hobbled, just as his hands were joined by a loop of rope.

"You, offspring of a braying jackal"—the lash, used by an expert, flicked him between shoulders already tender from such attentions—"go!"

Thus urged, he joined the line of march, though ahead of the unwieldy cage. Its stench gathered force in the heat, setting a cloud of evil odor about them. Cha-paz, on his feet now, strode with pride and importance as if he had never groveled before the official. Boxes and coffers, some of which Sherkarer recognized as part of the loot from Napata, were being carried by other slaves. A gilded statue wearing Amun-Ra's ram head, and a decorated chest—these could only have come from the palace of the Pharaoh.

The slaves who bore this loot were not Nubians. Sherkarer was the only one, and for that he was as humbled as if he had crawled on his belly before the white skins. He, of the Royal House, one wearing the Serpent, a slave to such as these! He was as one of the lions of the temple of Apedemek held by the triumphant enemy.

Sherkarer was startled at his thoughts. How dared he, one who had failed the Great God, who had not died bravely in battle but had come under the slave yoke, compare himself to the servants of Apedemek? Thoughts such as these might bring upon him the greater wrath of the Lion One! More words from the morning hymn came to him:

"The one who hurls his hot breath against the enemy
In this his name of great power.
The one who punishes all crimes committed against
  him—"

Those of Napata must have committed some great crime or Apedemek would not have turned his face from them.

The blaze of the sun, the pain in his shoulders where the whip had scored, his own hopeless fate, combined to make Sherkarer sick and dizzy, so that now and then he stumbled. Still he fought to keep on his feet, to march proudly as became a prince of Nubia in the hands of these barbarians.

As he went Sherkarer took less and less notice of his surroundings, until, at last, he was shoved into a room so dark that when the door was closed he could not see. No longer having to display pride, the captive fell to his knees and then lay upon the floor, staring up into the pressing dark. The walls must be thick, it was so cool here.

He wondered dully what would become of him now, whether he would end as one of the laborers who unloaded the ships. The slaves in Meroë, Napata—he had never considered them as people. They labored in the fields, or helped herd the cattle, or fetched and carried in the houses. But they had just been there, not of as much interest to their owners as a good hunting dog or a fine horse.

Had those slaves—the Egyptians taken in earlier wars, the wild black men from the south, the handful of captured mercenaries (strange, with fair hair and light eyes)—had they hated his people as he hated his present captors?

Far away was Napata, even farther Meroë. Perhaps he would never see them again, would be forced to live out his years in this hot, flat land. He closed his eyes and willed fiercely not to feel tears gather in them. He was Sherkarer, eldest son of the princess Bartare, of the blood of the great conqueror Piankhay, Pharaoh of the Two Lands, a noble of Nubia. But all that made no difference now. He was not a man grown, he was a boy who had not yet fronted a lion to be killed by his spear—and he was very much afraid.

He started out of a half-doze of misery as the door scraped open and the brightness of sunshine cut across the floor. A young man stood there and Sherkarer had to look at him under a shielding hand against the glare which hurt his eyes. He was no guard, he did not even have a knife in the folds of the soft sash around his waist.

On his cheeks was the beginning of a soft, curling beard, and his hair hung to his shoulders after the custom of these people—an unclean custom, for all men knew that it was better to shave head and body, and so keep fresher in the heat. The visitor was light of skin, too, lighter than an Egyptian. On his upper arms, between elbow and shoulder, he wore broad bands of silver. His sandals had colored toe and tie thongs, and his robe was blue, the sash woven of stripes, blue, green, yellow, with fringes at its ends.

Sherkarer rubbed one hand about the tattooed Serpent on his wrist, his one remaining sign of what he was, for his body was only scantily covered with a slave's waistcloth. He stared defiantly up at the young man in that rich dress. What was he doing here?

"I am named Daniel." The young man spoke slowly, a

little too loud, as if by that tone he could make a stupid stranger understand. Sherkarer did not resent his tone; he was too busy wondering if that odd name was really a name or some title among these barbarians. Did the newcomer expect him to throw himself on the floor and crawl?

The young man had turned, was taking a bowl and a jug from someone behind him who was too much in the glare of the courtyard for the Nubian to see. With these in his hands he came farther into the room, holding them out to Sherkarer.

"This is good." Again he spoke slowly, distinctly. "Eat and drink, brother."

The Nubian made no move to accept what was offered. "I am not your brother." He shaped the words with care, they were so different from either the Egyptian of the court or the Kushite tongue of the commoners. "I am Sherkarer, of the House of Piankhay!"

"Of Piankhay I have heard," the young man said. "He was king in Egypt once—"

"Pharaoh of the Two Lands! As his kinsman is now in Napata, in Meroë, in Nubia." Then he remembered only too well that in Napata there was now only death left.

"In Babylon there is only the Great King, Nebuchadnezzar," Daniel answered. "Though once in Jerusalem there was Jehoiakim of Judah, and then Zedekiah, who is now blind and captive here, to be mocked by the Great King. Kings are not always blessed with good fortune by Jehovah. But why do we speak of kings gone, brother? You must hunger and thirst, and this food is good. I have stood where you stand in this dark hour, and yet I still live. By the Lord God's favor, I have suffered no great ill, and have even won to some authority."

Sherkarer listened. Whether he could believe was another matter. It seemed that this Daniel meant good, and there was a deep hunger in him which made him tremble a little when he looked at the food. Still, he did not reach for the bowl, but looked searchingly at Daniel.

"Why do you come to me?"

"Because you are one taken from his home by war, even as I was. And—" He hesitated, and then spoke what Sherkarer thought to be the truth. "They say that you came with the dragon that has been given to the priests of Bel, and that you know much of it."

Sherkarer now took the food. He could more readily believe that it was brought in payment for information than because this stranger had merely shown general good will.

"I know of the lau," he answered shortly, determined that what he did not know he would invent, this being his only weapon against the city and its people.

"Lau—" Daniel repeated. "So do you call it in your tongue? Here they name it 'sirrush'—dragon. Men liken it to those demons seen only in evil dreams. Though there is an old, old tale that once such did abide in the river marshes, known to the priests of Bel, but that was in the far past.

"Now that Cha-paz has brought this sirrush-lau to the temple, it is taken to be a mighty omen in favor of Bel. It will give his priests even greater power—"

Sherkarer had been busy spooning the stew in the bowl into his mouth. It was good, far better fare than any he had had since the fall of Napata. But he was listening, too, for it is through the eyes and ears that one learns. A spiderweb of facts can tie up the lion of action; not to know is bad, not to strive to know is worse.

"Soon comes the time," Daniel was continuing, "when the great king Nebuchadnezzar himself must surrender all power to Marduk-Bel for a day, receiving it back only if the god chooses. To bring forth the sirrush-lau at such a ceremony will give the priests even more control."

"You speak of these priests and their god," Sherkarer interrupted, "as if they were not your priests, or your god."

The young man smiled. "There may be the chains of slavery on your wrists, brother, but no bonds lie upon your mind. No, all within Babylon know that I do not bow knee to Marduk-Bel, but serve the true God."

"Apedemek?" Sherkarer did not believe him.

Daniel shook his head. "The Lord God Jehovah, who made strong covenant with my people. We bow not in the temples of idols and false gods. And even here the Great King has listened to our words and has begun to seek for greater light than he can find on these cursed altars. But with the coming of this monster Marduk-Bel's priests wax stronger."

"The teeth smile, but what lies in the heart?" Sherkarer returned. "I eat by your favor, stranger, but wood may remain ten years in the river and still not become a crocodile. I do not see that I should take up sword in your war. What matters it to me what god this king calls upon?"

Still Daniel smiled. "You are weary and all is strange to you, even as it was when they brought us from Judea into Babylon. Perhaps I have been in too great haste in this matter. But you, even more than Cha-paz, know the nature of this sirrush. And the priests"—he lost his smile now, wearing the grim face of a warrior—"talk of giving a man as sacrifice to it. Do you not think that the first such offering might be you?"

"Thunder is not yet rain." Sherkarer tried to keep his voice steady. Some things he did know about the lau, and it could be that these priests could carry out such a sacrifice, though perhaps not just in the manner they intended. He was tired, and more than a little afraid. It was hard to play the warrior. Only let this stranger go so he could rest!

Then it was almost as if Daniel could read the thoughts in the Nubian's aching head, for he picked up the empty bowl, though he did not take the jug.

"Think on what I have said, brother. Time grows short. If you know anything concerning the sirrush which would be of aid in time of danger, you will do well to speak of it. The priests are the enemies of all who are not as they judge Bel's true sons. Times before have they tried to finish me, but by the power which lies in Jehovah's hand they have not triumphed. Nay, it has been made plain to all that Bel is the lesser. So now the priests look afield for aught they can summon to impress upon those here the greatness of their god. This dragon, they think, can be used thus. I have the favor of the Great King at present, but such is short-lived, and one must make the most of it while it lasts."

He went out, leaving the door a little open. Sherkarer could see the shadow of a guard standing there. Not that he could hope to escape with the hobbles upon him. Raising the jug, he drank. It was thin, sour, barley beer and he made a face over it, though it was good to have something to wet his dry throat. He fingered the tattoo of Apedemek's sign on his wrist. This Daniel with all his talk of strange gods— It was plain that though he walked free in this mighty temple he was not one with those who held it, but also a captive from another land, though he had won to some favor with the King.

That such favor could be fleeting he did not have to warn Sherkarer. In Nubia that was also true. Men rose by the smiles of the Pharaoh and the Candace, or fell by their frowns. This Daniel, he must be a brave man to do as he was doing, to come into the house of his enemies, seek out a captive there to ask for help in the undoing of those same enemies—for he was sure now that that had been Daniel's purpose.

A man with too much ambition does not sleep in peace —was that it? Was Daniel moved by ambition? Sherkarer closed his eyes. He had been an unscarred boy when he went to Napata, now he looked back at those days as if they were years away. Though he did not wear the marks of the lion claws on his face, he was now a man, and one who needed to use all his wits in order to live.

Was life as a slave worth the living? Better it would be to face the lau after all—if the lau still lived. Cha-paz had had a hard enough time keeping the creature breathing during the journey. Water it needed, and the green stuff to fill its belly. For though the creature looked like an eater of man and beast, it did not mouth meat. However, it would kill—horribly—even the hippopotamus or the lion were it angered.

Its strong hind legs were clawed with talons like a bird's, its shorter forearms were able to rend and tear. The lashing tail could sweep a man, or horse, or lion, off his feet. The long neck supported a serpentlike head, frilled as a lizard's, but with a horn on the tip of the nose, which it used for rooting out the swamp plants it craved. Kept too much in the sun, or too hot, it became feeble and near to dying. When they had taken it to Napata they had had to wet down the reed mats hung about its cage. It appeared that in the day's heat it was used to taking to the water, coming forth only at night.

Cha-paz had been in Napata before the Egyptians had come. Sherkarer suspected that when the merchant came out of hiding to bid for the spoil looted by the mercenaries, he had acted as a spy. It was not the first time that the King of Kings, the lord of Babylon, had reached greedy fingers into Nubia. But before, when his own army had marched that way, they had found the journey such that not even a remnant of them had been left to cross into Kush.

It was Cha-paz who had prevented the slaying of the lau by the enemy's archers, who had been ready to shoot it as a demon. He must have given a small fortune to bring it hither. Likewise, he had sought out Sherkarer among the captives when he learned that the monster had been brought to Napata by the men of Meroë, and that the boy was the only one left of that band.

So far had the Nubian traced his way into the past when another visitor arrived. This time it was Cha-paz himself, flanked by two of his overseers.

Sherkarer was given no explanation as he was brought forth from the room and taken across the courtyard into another building, where other slaves took charge of him, wrenching away his waistcloth, standing him on a runneled square of tile, pouring jars of water over his thin body, rubbing him with oil and sand. Then they threw him a single short garment, waist-belted with a strip of scarlet cloth.

During the journey from Nubia his hair had grown into a short, fuzzy bristle on his shaven head, but they did not offer him the comfort of a fresh shaving. And certainly he had no wig of ceremony.

He was taken forth and shown to Cha-paz, who walked about him, staring him up and down as if he were not alive, or a man, but a thing of the merchant's own creation. The Nubian balled his fingers into a fist, but willed himself as best he could to give no sign of the hate within him.

"Listen, you." The merchant took a stand directly before Sherkarer. "It is said that the heart of a god is as far away as the center of heaven. Even farther will you find the mercy of him you are to serve here, if you disobey. I could have left you to be eaten by the vultures now feasting in Napata. For if you think that the soldiers of the true Pharaoh would have allowed you who wear that mark"—he pointed to the tattoo—"to live long you are stupid. That you are not dead is by my choice, and that you continue to live is also by my will. You live for but one reason: you helped bring the sirrush to Napata, and so you know more of it than any man still living. What you know you shall tell us, and the keepers of the sirrush shall you serve."

So Sherkarer became a part of the temple of Marduk-Bel, attached to the three priests chosen to attend the sirrush. And he used his new position as best he could.

The temple was like a city in itself, with many courtyards and buildings. The rich inner chapel was overlaid with gold, wherein stood the images of Marduk and his wife, Saparatum (together with smaller statues of their attendants), with no sparing of either precious metal or jewels. But into that room only the Great King and the highest ranking of the priests might enter.

In one of the courtyards those in command of the sirrush partially roofed over a pool with a matting of daily-refreshed reeds and vines. There they housed their dragon, bringing vegetation to tempt the monster. But it was sluggish and showed only faint interest in its surroundings. Sherkarer, to preserve his image of one expert on dragon matters, squatted on the border of the pool, though the foul odor of the creature made him sick, for hours at a time, as if it were important that he keep strict vigil.

Twice he had seen the young man Daniel, though they had not spoken together again. But he learned from the slaves how much he was hated by the priests. It was true that he had been a war captive, even as Sherkarer, coming from a small country to the west. It had been the whim of Ashpezaa, the Vizir, to select certain of the fairest of the captive children to be raised in his service. And among those Daniel was the leader.

Strange tales were told of him: that he had been put into the den of the King's lions, after those had been kept hungry, yet none had touched him. He had challenged the priests and had proved that no god came at night to touch the sacrifice left on the altar; rather, it was taken away by men who left plain tracks in the ashes Daniel had caused to be strewn secretly before the altar.

Now Nebuchadnezzar, the Great King, listened to Daniel and his talk of a single God who held all power. And therefore the priests sought a way of pulling him down.

Several times the High Priest himself, as great a power within this sprawling temple town as the King was without, sent his chief scribe to look upon the sirrush and talk privately with its keepers. Sherkarer did not doubt they were hatching some plan in which the dragon was to play a part. But he was well aware now that upon the sirrush depended his own life. He had no value to his captors except that he knew, or rather pretended to know, more about the monster than they did.

And he was a prisoner indeed in the compound which housed it, for there were always guards by the single gate. No one came or went save that he carried a tablet impressed with the High Priest's seal.

It was on the tenth day after Sherkarer had been taken to the temple that one of the slaves, come to clear away the withered vegetation of the pool screen and bring a new supply, appeared to stumble to one knee by Sherkarer. Something small flew from his hand, came to a stop beside the Nubian's sandal. When the man did not move to reach for it, Sherkarer set his foot upon it. After the slave was gone he stooped as if to tighten the ankle thong of his footwear, and his fingers closed upon what the other had lost.

His heart gave such a leap as he looked upon what lay cupped in his palm, yet he was afraid he might have betrayed himself. Yet, as he hastily looked around, there was no one near save the slave laborers, and the temple overseer was watching only them.

A precious thing out of the past, a part of what must have been the loot of Napata—a lapis scarab bearing the name of Piankhay himself. Why? Were there more Nubians here in Babylon? Men who had heard of Sherkarer, though he did not know of them? If so, they must also be slaves—yet they had taken the risk of trying to reach him.

He saw that the same slave who had dropped the scarab was returning. There was no chance to question him. The man had scooped up an armload of the rotting stuff, and as he passed Sherkarer a whisp of it shifted out of his load.

The Nubian kicked it to one side, wondering how he could discover what he must know from the messenger. Then he saw that one of the reeds was fresher, greener, than the rest—and had marks upon it. He kicked at it again, sending it from the side of the pool into some shade, and went there to sit cross-legged, watching the workmen as he had done many times before. His hands closed upon that piece of reed; he began to twist it idly this way and that.

All the while he was straining to read those marks. At last he made out a few signs. They were rudely scratched, written as if someone who knew only a little court Egyptian had made them. That did not mean that a fellow Nubian could not have written them. Very few except court scribes could any longer write so with ease.

"Midday—west wall—water channel—" He thought that was the message.

There was a water channel at the foot of the left wall, a pipe laid down through which the water of the pool could be drained if necessary. At midday the courtyard would be near-deserted, since all sensible men sought the cool and shade of the thick-walled inner rooms. Sherkarer found himself swallowing; moisture filled his mouth as well as standing in beads upon his forehead and upper lip and making the palms of his hands slippery.

Escape—surely this must mean escape! And though he had seen no chance for that, perhaps others had been more fortunate. Who could they be? Some of the guard who had survived the storming of the Candace's palace, even some of her nobles? Those who knew his high birth might be willing to risk much for him. It could even be, if the Pharaoh had not reached the safety of Meroë, that Sherkarer's own family now ruled Nubia. Such speculations made him restless, so that he could not sit and wait, but arose and walked around the edge of the pool. The waters were murky, evil-smelling, as always, and the sirrush-lau had sunk to the bottom, seeking a hiding place from the light which struck in while the matting was being replaced.

The Nubian tried to measure by the shadows how much time it might be before his appointed meeting. He fought down his excitement and he was lucky in that there was no senior priest on duty. The others were so used to his daily inspection of the pool, which he made last as long as possible to suggest his special knowledge, that they no longer watched him.

He ate alone, as usual, for here he was neither slave laborer nor freeman. So he drew his ration of barley-meal porridge, radishes, a few figs, and today an onion. These he ate very quickly, hardly able to choke down the mouthfuls.

Midday—and the courtyard was empty. Sherkarer walked to the pool, appearing to check on the new matting roof. He could hear from beyond the wall the trumpeting of an ill-tempered elephant. The sound carried well, since the usual hum of the temple and the city had died away. A swift glance told him he was unobserved as he came to the drain, squatting down there to look as if he suspected some trouble with the water supply.

"You are there?" A voice came hollowly out of the ground.

But the three words were enough to disappoint the Nubian. No countryman of his would speak so; his own hard-learned knowledge of this language carried with it an accent, and he was sure that the same would be true of any Nubian.

"I am here," he answered, wanting to solve the mystery of who had sent a royal scarab, pricked a message on a reed.

There was a grunt, as if whoever lay there was trying to shift position in cramped quarters. Then the other spoke again. "Have you thought of the words of Daniel, Nubian?"

Daniel! Was that court intriguer still trying to draw him into some plot against the priests?

"He who asks questions cannot avoid answers in turn" —Sherkarer repeated a country saying as he tried to think fast. "Who are you who hide in the ground to speak of Daniel?"

"One who is his ears and sometimes his mouth, when there is need for it, Nubian." But the voice was impatient now. "I ask again—have you thought upon his words?"

"Why should I, hidden one? One who runs alone cannot be outrun by another. I live because the sirrush lives, and they believe that I know that which keeps it so."

"Would you then choose to remain here as a slave to a stinking monster when you could be free and on the trail back to your own country?"

"Restless feet may carry one into a snake pit—"

"I have no time to trade wise sayings with you, Nubian! This is an offer, take it or throw it away. Support Daniel that he may win the full favor of the King, or else remain as you are until your monster dies and you have no longer a place here. Daniel forgets not those who stand with him—and the might of the Great King's seal reaches across the world. He can win your freedom and an open road to your own land."

"If he can do this," retorted Sherkarer, "then why has he not done so for himself? He said with his own mouth that he is captive here. One falsehood spoils a thousand truths, hole lurker!"

"There is laid upon Daniel a task, set by the Lord God Jehovah—that he abide here to soften the heart of the Great King toward our people. He chooses Babylon to serve." The voice sounded so much in earnest that the Nubian's doubt was shaken.

"A man can promise the world, yet when the time comes he may be unable to give even a pinch of dust. You would dangle the hope of freedom and Meroë before me as one coaxes a donkey with a bunch of fine grass—yet the eating of that grass may never come."

"How long will your monster live, Nubian? Measure your own life-span by its! If it dies here, will the priests let the blame rest upon them? Not when they have a slave to name."

That was a hard truth which hit home as might a well-aimed arrow. The creature was sluggish and had been

94

showing less and less activity lately. It could well be that the thing would not live long here. And of course he would get the blame when it died. His own efforts to be considered an expert on the care of the sirrush would stand against him then.

"What does Daniel want of me?" he asked. There was no harm in knowing that much.

"Tell him what the creature feeds upon most readily. He has challenged the priests, that he may slay the dragon by his will alone, using no sword, or spear, or arrow— And he has but two days in which to make ready. Does the creature attack men?"

"If it is angered, yes. And it can slay, easily and in a horrible fashion. Two days ago it was alarmed by the braying of a donkey that brought in the guards' beer. It tore the poor beast to pieces."

"Can the priests incite it to such behavior?"

"They might." Sherkarer was not sure how, but he believed that the priests would make a challenge from Daniel an excuse to do their utmost to see that he died as the result of his folly.

"Then—what does it feed upon most readily? Can you find a bit of that?"

"There is a reed root which it seeks out first among that offered it. I do not know the name but—"

"Get a handful of it. Have it ready tomorrow and lay it in the matting to be taken away. On the next day, in the morning, when the fodder is brought, there will be in it a ball with those roots fixed to its outer part. See that this is ready near the top of the creature's food pile."

"And if I do?" But there was no answer, though Sherkarer took the chance of lying flat and calling softly through the grating of the drain. Whoever had been there was now gone. He went back to his own quarters to think.

The unseen person had promised much. But it all depended upon *ifs*—if he was able to supply a sample of root, if Daniel could use it in some way, if Sherkarer could survive the fury of the priests should Daniel actually slay the beast; if Daniel kept his promise and, winning the king's favor, remembered the Nubian. If and if and if—

On the other hand, if the sirrush died, then he could look forward only to certain death, and probably not an easy one. Sherkarer thought that on either hand he faced a dark future. But it was better perhaps to do as Daniel's man suggested. What one hopes for is always better than what one has.

So he followed orders, seeing that a handful of root went out with the discarded matting. He was glad he had done so when at night the sirrush only nibbled a little of what was offered it.

"The beast ails." The chief priest in the compound turned on Sherkarer and there was a harsh note in his voice. "What is the matter with it?"

"It is still tired from that long journey when it had not the proper food or water," Sherkarer hurried to say. "Now that it is here it will speedily become well again."

"It had better, black face, or else you shall find what is done to those who ill serve Marduk-Bel. And tomorrow—" He hesitated and then added, "Tomorrow it must be ready to take vengeance upon an enemy of our God. It must come forth from the water and strike down him who denies the will of Marduk. How can this be done?"

"If men stand at the other end of the pool"—Sherkarer had already given some thought to this, for any plan Daniel might have would surely fail if the beast continued to sulk under the surface of the water—"and strike the water with poles, then it will come into this shallow end. Also this must be done in the evening, for it hates

96

the day as you know. And most of the torches must be kept at the far end."

He was trying to remember the story of how the thing had been captured in the first place. He was sure it had been driven into the pit cage in this fashion.

"It shall be done." The priest nodded to the scribe waiting for orders.

The next morning Sherkarer found the ball of reeds in one of the baskets of vegetation. From it came the smell of pitch and fat, and small hairs stuck out among the reeds, so that he rolled it in a second covering and laid it just under the surface of the food pile. The rest of the day he clung to patience, a hundred times ready to go and knock away that ball, sure that he could not trust Daniel or his plans; and a hundred times he remained where he was because he had that thin thread of hope.

When the dusk came those making this trial came, and with them the Great King himself. They set a throne for him so that he was raised high above his guards and courtiers. The High Priest had a lesser throne to his right, while a row of guards made a wall between them and the pool. Sherkarer was crowded back against the wall, but he had kicked together a pile of reeds and stood high enough on the unstable footing to be able to see.

The matting roof was torn away, and then the priest who had charge of the sirrush made a gesture. There was a beating of drums and a calling of rams' horns, while slaves with poles struck the water of the pool, two rows of torches behind them.

The water became covered with a murky froth raised by their efforts. Then the head of the sirrush rose on its snake neck. It gave a honking cry, louder than Sherkarer had ever heard before, and its head darted back and forth as might that of a serpent preparing to strike. Then it turned away from those tormenting it by curdling the water. Since the other end of the pool was shallow it arose, standing now upon its powerful hind legs, its forepaws curled a little against its belly, its head forward.

A man came up on the steps before the Great King, and though the torchers here were but few Sherkarer saw he was Daniel. As he came the King's hand rose in a signal, and at that moment all the clamor made by the horns, the drums, the beating of the water, was stilled, so that Daniel's voice could be heard as it carried clearly across the courtyard.

"Oh, King, live forever! I have come to judgment with your god. As I have said, I carry no weapon—" He spread his hands wide that all men could see they were empty. "Yet shall I slay this beast even as if I thrust him through with the blade of the King's own sword. And I shall slay him through the power of the Lord God Jehovah, who has willed me to come hither, into this place of false gods."

There was a stir among the priests, a murmur, but again the King's hand brought silence.

Then Daniel turned and went to the poolside. The beast was taller than two such men as it reared, awaiting him. And now even the angry swaying of its head was stilled. Sherkarer drew a deep breath, his eyes on its tail, waiting for the betraying quiver which would mean that that scaled and terrible lash would strike down this defenseless man.

Yet Daniel walked as one without fear, his hands up, palms outward. And from his lips came words the Nubian could not understand. But he guessed that the other called upon this God of his in his own tongue. The words rolled as a chant of a priest. Upon hearing them the priests of Marduk-Bel moved as if they would rush this outlander who so profaned their temple.

Now it was the High Priest who raised his hand to quiet them. Sherkarer tensed, for he thought he saw a quiver run along the beast's tail.

Still it did not move and the Nubian began to believe that Daniel was weaving a spell with that chant, was holding the monster so. Then, still speaking, Daniel picked up a handful of the reed roots. These he bunched together into a ball and tossed into the air. The monster's jaws gaped, caught that mass of vegetation, crunched it.

Sherkarer was frozen with amazement. That the creature would eat so at Daniel's offering he could hardly believe, even though he had seen it with his own eyes.

A second time Daniel fed the sirrush with a tossed bundle of roots. Around him no man moved or made a sign. So still was the whole company that the Nubian could hear the breathing of the men beside him.

For the third time Daniel took up a ball of food. This time Sherkarer was sure it was that which he had hidden among the roots at Daniel's bidding. And for the third time the monster accepted the offering, crunched, and swallowed.

But this time the root ball held that poisonous offering prepared by Daniel's people, so it was as if the lau had swallowed one of the torches. It arched backward, giving voice in deep bellows. The tail lashed and fell, lashed and fell, whipping the water again into froth, yet not reaching any enemy, for all pressed quickly away from the rim of the pool. Then, with an effort they could see, it tried to reach Daniel, who had not retreated more than a step or two. Instead it collapsed, to writhe and kick, its horned serpent head resting on the poolside. And so it died.

Then Daniel turned to face the Great King.

"Oh, King, live forever"—he gave the ceremonious salute. "Is it not as I have promised? With the aid of the

99

Lord God Jehovah, this evil monster, which was servant to the priests of darkness, is dead. Yet I did not draw steel against it, only fed it its natural food."

And the Great King reached forth his scepter of state so that Daniel could set his fingertips to it. There was a sigh throughout the company, and men suddenly found their voices, speaking one to the other in awe and wonder of what they had seen. But the priests gathered together in a tight knot about the throne of their chief, and their faces were flushed with anger.

Sherkarer flattened himself against the wall, trying to hide behind the courtiers. He had done this thing for Daniel, and now—what reason was there for the other to remember a Nubian captive? Let him be left to the priests and they would undoubtedly wreak upon him their hatred for this stranger who had so demeaned their god.

A hand fell upon his shoulder, and he swung about, ready to fight, if without any chance, against the man who held him so. But the low voice in his ear he had heard before, out of the drain.

"Throw this about you, walk beside me, but hurry not." The other had one of the richly fringed shawls which the nobles used as cloaks, and he pulled it quickly about Sherkarer.

Thus, as one of the Great King's household the Nubian left that well-guarded courtyard, the temple itself. And he followed in the train of courtiers back across the river to the western side, where stood the newly built palace, to be lost in the maze of servant quarters there.

It was a day and a night before Daniel came to him. But in his hand was a hard-baked clay tablet he gave to the Nubian.

"Take care—this bears the Great King's seal print. Now, at the wharf is the ship of the merchant Balzar.

Also there is this—" And he took from the folds of his sash a small bag. "This holds pieces of trade silver, enough, I hope, to get you home."

Sherkarer weighed the bag in one hand, the King's passport in the other, his keys to freedom. He asked a last question. "How was it that you knew the lau would eat what you offered it?"

"Did I not say I was bearing witness to the power of the Lord God Jehovah? It was by *His* will the beast ate."

The Nubian tucked the bag of silver into the front of the plain short robe his guide had supplied.

"Your God is a mighty one, but he has also done another thing. He brought me to be your servant when I had no wish to be so. In that much will I also bear witness to His might. I wish you well, Daniel, but I am glad that I shall do it distantly. You and your God together are such as might bring down a kingdom if it be your will."

"Not my will, but *His*," Daniel corrected him. "And perhaps that shall also happen."

And later, in Meroë of the south, Sherkarer heard the tale of how Babylon the mighty had been taken, wall and tower, palace and temple, by the Persians, and he wondered whether Daniel and his God had had a hand in that.

4

PENDRAGON

Ras was not looking at the sirrush-lau writhing at the poolside. He saw instead the flat picture of a queer creature as it might have been drawn by men who had heard the monster described but had not seen it in all its horrible might. His hand lay so that the fingers touched the edge of the puzzle, but he saw no blue tattoo marks forming a bracelet about his wrist. Drawing a deep breath, he pushed back from the table.

Had it all been a dream? But it was far too real. Why, he had been hungry, and tired, and frightened—he could remember every detail of the adventure as if it were all true. He was Sherkarer of Meroë, not George Brown of Sedgwick Manor!

What if he had not listened to Daniel or helped in the plan to defeat the priests of Marduk-Bel? What if the sirrush-lau had died naturally and they had blamed him for it? Ras shivered. He knew he had chosen rightly, for him, and for Daniel, too. He remembered that Daniel was in the Bible, but he did not remember the dragon story.

Ras looked for the last time at the blue dragon fitted firmly together. He did not in the least want to finish the rest of the puzzle. Somehow he could not bring himself to even touch it now.

Time! He had forgotten all about time! The clothes at the laundromat—Mom waiting for them! How long had he been here? In his dream it had been days—days! Only it could not really have been that long—

Frightened now, he ran back through the dusty rooms,

the old floorboards creaking under him as he went. He pushed out of the window, letting it bang down behind him, and ran down the rutted, leaf-filled drive. Ras reached the laundromat puffing and went straight to the right machine.

"Better watch it, son." Mr. Reese was standing there. "Your wash was done about ten minutes ago. Other people waiting to use these, you ought to stay right here."

"Sorry," Ras said breathlessly. He jerked out his basket, unloaded the clothes to take them to the dryers at the other end, trying to keep his mind on what he was doing.

Mr. Reese followed along behind. "No running off this time, boy. You keep your eyes on this and empty it as soon as it's done, mind. Too many people waiting on Saturday's to tie up machines needlessly."

"Yes, sir," Ras mumbled as he pushed the damp wash in as fast as he could, then hunted for the change to feed into the dryer. The laundromat was crowded, not only with ladies but with men and boys, too.

Ras caught sight of a familiar face, Sig Dortmund. Sig was leaning against the wall and he had a book in his hand, not a paperback or a comic but a real book. It was from the library, Ras thought, for it had a protective plastic jacket on. And as Sig turned a little to let by a lady with two big bags of wash, Ras saw that jacket more clearly. There was a picture of a man with long yellow hair over his shoulders in braids. He had a big hammer raised high in one hand, and in the other was a sword laid out on a narrow rest, as if he were ready to pound it with the hammer.

Sig was so intent upon his book that he did not look up as Ras edged closer.

Story of Sigurd—Ras read the title.

Though he had not spoken the words aloud, Sig suddenly looked up as if he had heard. He looked at Ras and flushed.

"Hi." His voice sounded as if he were not sure he ought to talk to Ras. Then he added in a rush of words, "I went back, to let you out. I didn't want you to have to stay down there. Only, you were gone."

Ras nodded. "I know, I saw you go. . . . Listen." He moved closer so that he could ask his questions without anyone overhearing him. "You put together the silver dragon, didn't you? Well, when you did—did anything queer happen then?"

For a moment he thought that Sig was not going to answer. The other boy looked away, at the dryer as if he must check it, then at the book he held. Ras, uneasy, was ready to move off again, when Sig spoke. "Yeah. Something happened."

"You—you went to Babylon—and Daniel was there?" Ras asked.

Sig stared at him in open surprise. "Babylon? Daniel? You're crazy, man. I went with Sigurd, to help kill Fafnir —for the treasure. Sigurd killed him. But then he wouldn't take the treasure, he said it made a man go bad. It did Mimir, and he was Sigurd's friend before. So that must have been true."

Now it was Ras's turn to be bewildered. "Sigurd," he repeated. "But—that's the book you're reading."

"I didn't even know there was a book about it—until I saw this when we had library period yesterday. But it's wrong in some parts: Sig Clawhand isn't in the story at all. And he was part of it. I know because I was him—I was!" He looked at Ras as if challenging him to deny that.

"And you put the silver dragon together," Ras said slowly. "So you had one story. I put the blue one together, and I had another story—they were not the same at all."

"The blue one!" Sig no longer held the book open with his finger between the pages to keep his place. He gave all his attention to Ras. "You did the blue one—and then you had an adventure. Where?" His demand was sharp and eager.

Ras hesitated. The adventure was so real, so much a part of his memory, that he almost did not want to share it. But there was the mystery of what had happened to both of them. Perhaps if they compared stories they could discover what was in the puzzle which made them see and feel— If Sig had seen and felt as he, Ras, had done.

"I was in a war—in Africa, I think." He made it as simple as possible. "And there was this big thing out of the swamps. My people called it 'lau,' but the priests of Babylon called it 'sirrush.' A merchant took it and me to Babylon. And there the temple priests made me help take care of it." Swiftly he outlined his adventure.

When he had finished Sig looked thoughtful. "Daniel's in the Bible, so he was real, once. But I don't remember hearing that dragon story before. Listen, on Monday, why don't you go to the library as I did, see if you can find a book about it? I know about Egypt; heck, we studied all about that—pyramids, mummies—last year. But I never heard of this Meroë place, or Nap—Napata"— he stumbled over the strange name. "But if you could find it written down, it might prove it *was* all true. There's a part in this book, at the front"—Sig turned the pages hurriedly—"where it says that maybe there was a real Sigurd. Only, after he was dead people added a lot of extra things to the story, because he was a hero they liked to talk about. So now he's more like a made-up person.

Only, he wasn't! I know!" Sig's chin was up. He looked at Ras as if he dared him to question that.

"Daniel was real and so was Sherkarer. Even if I can't find him in any book," Ras said. "But I'm going to look—"

"This your wash, boy?" A lady with a scarf tied over bumps of curlers pushed up to Sig.

"Yes, ma'am." Sig shoved his book under his belt and hurried to empty the dryer, while the lady gave impatient little snorts to urge him along. Ras went to check on his machine, not wanting Mr. Reese to speak to him again. As he left, Sig looked up.

"See you—"

"Sure," Ras returned.

There were still ten minutes to go on the dryer. He saw Sig bag his wash and go out. But before he left he looked at Ras and gave a little salute with his hand. Ras stirred from one foot to another impatiently.

Sig had found a book written about his adventure. Was there one about Ras's, too? When he got home he would write down all the names he could remember. And he would get the Bible and read the part about Daniel. Though he was sure that if there were a dragon he would remember from having heard it in Sunday school. Daniel in the lions' den, that was a story he had heard several times when he was a little kid. And Sherkarer had heard the slaves talk about it in Babylon.

And if Napata and Meroë weren't in the Bible, then maybe he could find them in a history book. He had never tried looking up things, except what he had to do for school. But this was different, more exciting, because he had been a part of it. Shaka was always talking about Africa and how people said black men didn't have any real history, but they had. Did one of those leaflets and books Shaka was always getting have something about

Meroë and the black Pharaohs like Piankhay and—Ras was impatient to get home and look at his brother's library. Suddenly it was taking forever to get the drying done.

Another thought crossed Ras's mind. Sig had put together the silver dragon, and he had done the blue one. But there were two more, the red and the gold ones. What adventures could they have with them?

When Ras returned home Mom was not in the kitchen doing the usual Saturday morning baking (Mom liked to make her own cakes—from scratch, she said—not use mixes except when she was in a big hurry). Instead she sat in the living room and she was crying. Dad stood at the window, his back to the room, his hands in his pockets. The very set of his shoulders said he was good and mad.

"He's of age," Dad was saying as Ras came in. "And he's so set in this madness that you can't argue with him! But I won't have that kind of lawless talk in this house—understand, Louise?"

Mom did not answer, she just went on crying. And Ras felt sick to his stomach, as he always did when Mom got so upset. Neither one of them looked at him when he came in with the clean laundry, and he was more uneasy than ever. It was as if they had forgotten all about him. Finally he had to say something.

"Got the clothes back, Mom."

But it was Dad who turned to look at him. "George!" His voice showed that he was really upset, and it looked as though it was Ras who had upset him this time. The boy tried to think of what he had done. The old house—the puzzle—that must be it! And he had no excuse, either. He felt sicker than ever.

"I understand you have been refusing to answer to

your proper name at school." Dad crossed the room to stand over him.

Ras was so surprised at the accusation, which was so far from what he expected, that he had no quick answer.

"Your brother is both foolish and stubborn," Dad continued. "I am not going to have you copy him, understand! Your name is George Brown and nothing else—no African mumbo-jumbo! And he is Lloyd Brown. If I catch you repeating any of his dangerous and stupid remarks, I'll see that you don't do it again. Your brother has just about broken your mother's heart. You look at her—look at her good, boy! Do you want her to cry like that over you? Do you?" Dad's voice was close to a roar.

"No—no, sir," Ras found an answer. What had Shaka —Lloyd—done?

"You had better remember that! Your brother has chosen his own way. He's left this house and he is not coming back as long as he talks the kind of treasonable rubbish he spouted out this morning! I served my country" —Dad ran his hands over his face and then rubbed his forehead as if he had a bad ache behind it—"I did not want to go in the army, very few men do. But there was a war on and I believed in what we were fighting for. I'm not an African—I'm an American, and I'm proud of it— proud, do you understand! And I'm not going to have treason talked in this house! I only hope Lloyd will come to his senses in time. He has a good brain, why doesn't he use it?"

Dad went back to the window. Mom wiped her eyes on a tissue from her apron pocket. "He's a good boy underneath all that foolishness, Evan. He'll come back, I know he will. I—well, it just surprised me so, his saying he was going to live with that awful Ali man. I guess I was shaken up. But I know it will all come out all right— Lloyd's a good boy."

Dad made some kind of a noise and Mom got up and went to stand beside him, her hand on his shoulder. Ras swallowed, picked up the laundry bag. So Shaka had left as he had threatened to do. Ras had seen Ali once—a thin man with a little pointed beard and a quick, angry want of talking. He was the one who had started Shaka reading all the African books.

Those books! Had Shaka taken them with him? Ras left the clothes in the hall and slipped upstairs. Shaka's room was bare, except that his closet door was open and hanging inside was his good suit, the one he hardly ever wore any more. There was a drawer pulled crookedly out of the bureau, but it was empty. And there were light places on the wall where his posters had been. Yes, the bookshelf was bare.

Ras sat down on the edge of the bed. That sick feeling which had started at seeing Mom cry was worse. Shaka had gone. Dad said he was wrong, stupid. But when his brother had talked about what he believed, he could make you believe it, too. Or almost—because Dad's arguments were just as strong. It was like Sherkarer's belief in Apedemek and Daniel's in the Lord God Jehovah.

But Ras knew one thing: Sherkarer had gained his freedom because he had trusted in a man of another religion and race. They had worked together to destroy the sirrush-lau; neither could have done it alone. Working together— Like Sig and he. Last time, in the old house, they had fought and Sig had locked him in the basement. But today they had had something in common.

Now he wanted to see Sig again—talk about those two other dragons. And it was easier to think about that than about Shaka and what was happening here at home.

Artie Jones kicked the football so that it hit the curb and bounced back. He picked it up, saw its new brown side was already scuffed. He had done that himself, just fooling around with it. What was the use of having a football if you didn't have any guys to play with? Nobody lived around here but that kook Kim Stevens, and Sig Dortmund, and that Ras guy. He did not want to get hooked up with them, not when there were smooth guys like Greg Ross and his gang around. He had hoped they would suggest kicking when he took his ball to school yesterday. But they had been so busy talking about how they were all going to the Senior High game this afternoon that they had not heard him say he had a new ball or even looked his way when he got it out of the locker to show them.

Greg's dad was taking them in the station wagon, and they sure would have a groovy time. Artie had stood there, hoping, just a little, that Greg would turn around and ask him to go, too.

Nothing much to do around here—never was. He could go down to the movies. But he'd seen the picture they had this week. And the TV was at the repair shop. If he hung around home Mom would ask about doing homework. He sure was not going to spend Saturday doing that!

There was Sig heading to the corner in a hurry. If they played ball here, though, Sig would expect to hang around with him at school, too. Then Artie might never get a chance to be one of Greg's gang. Only, it sure was lonesome. Halfheartedly Artie began to walk down the block after Sig.

Sig did not look in his direction at all. Was he going back to the old house? Suppose he was? It was a spooky place but exciting. Had Sig found something in that locked room? Artie had not asked him. Now he wondered. But Sig was waiting there at the corner. Not for Artie, he never turned around to see him. No, he was waving at someone on the other side of the street. Why, it was that dopey kid who wouldn't tell his right name. What was Sig doing with *him?*

Artie trailed half a block behind the other two, who had joined forces. Yes, they were heading for the old house. They had stopped by the wall, were looking around. Moved by an impulse he did not understand, Artie crouched down behind a rubbish can. It did not hide him very well, but he guessed they did not see him, for they were going on in. Suddenly he was determined to follow them. If Sig had found something he should have told Artie, not that dope! After all, Artie had been with him that first time. Maybe Sig thought Artie was too chicken because he had not stayed. Well, he would go in behind them, see what they had found, then let them know he'd watched them. That would show Sig!

He watched Sig climb through the window, Ras slipping in after him. Artie, still holding the football, followed. They had a flashlight, he did not. But today there was enough light for him to find his way. He heard the murmur of their voices, but not their words.

They had gone right to the room Sig had wanted to open that first time. Artie slipped along the wall of the hall as quietly as he could, trying to hear.

"Heads takes the red—that fair?" Sig asked.

"Right!"

There was a moment of silence and then Sig said, with disappointment, "Tails. Well, are you going to try?"

There was another period of quiet and then Artie heard Ras say in a very excited voice, "You saw that, didn't you? It—it moved right away from my fingers!"

"Let me try!" Sig sounded impatient.

"See? It does that for you, too!"

"Let's try the yellow one then."

114

Red what? Yellow what? Artie was so curious he almost went to the doorway to see.

"It's no good," Sig said. "That first time, the pieces went together as if they wanted to, like I was hardly working at it. Was it the same for you?"

"Yes. But now it won't. See, I can't even hold a piece, it slips right away from me. Sig, do you suppose that means we are not going to be able to finish it?"

"But why not? What good is it only half done? There is no reason—"

"There might be one we don't know. I—I think we ought to leave it alone now, Sig, I really do."

"It's darn queer. Maybe it's just today, maybe if we came back some other time—"

"Maybe, Sig, but somehow I don't think so. And don't you feel queer now, as if we shouldn't be here at all? I didn't feel that way before."

There was a long moment of quiet and then Sig answered, "Yeah. I wasn't going to say that, you might think I was a kook or something. But—let's get out of here—right now!"

Artie was confused. Somehow he did not want to face them at this moment. He looked around a little wildly, tugged open the nearest door, and swung into a closet, keeping his hand on the doorknob and the door open a crack. He did not even see them go by, but he heard their footsteps echoing through the big rooms. When it was quiet again he came out, determined to see what was in the room, what this red-yellow thing might be.

At first glance he saw nothing at all but a table and a chair. Then the light from the window showed him color on the table, which drew him closer.

The football dropped from his loosened grasp and he was not even aware he had lost it. A puzzle—a jigsaw puzzle! Why had Sig and Ras been so excited about a stupid old puzzle? There was a box there, too, with a lot of pieces in it. Some were turned up to show brilliant red or gleaming gold. There were a few red pieces lying by themselves to one side. How they glowed!

He could see the picture on the lid of the box, with a big silver dragon at the top and a queer blue one at the bottom, just like the finished two on the table. Then there were two more, a red dragon on the left and a gold one on the right. He hardly looked at the gold one. It was the red which caught his full attention.

It was—it looked so real! Artie put out a finger and touched one of the red pieces. It moved a little and—why, it actually seemed to snap into place beside another, interlocking smoothly. But Sig and Ras, they had talked as if they couldn't get the pieces together at all! What did they mean—this was easy!

One of the pieces was lying face down and there was black writing on it, the letters thick and blocky. "R-e-x—Rex," Artie spelled out.

Uncle Jim had had a dog named Rex once, he said it meant "king" in Latin.

Artie flipped the piece over. Yes, it went in here. Say, this was smooth. He began to sort out the rest of the red pieces. Why, he could do this, even if Ras and Sig could not. This went here, and that there— Forgetting everything else, Artie settled down in the chair.

Red dragon, a red dragon up against a blue sky—Pendragon! That was it, he knew it as well as if someone standing at his elbow had told him—the Pendragon!

ARTOS, SON OF MARIUS

It was harvest time and most of the war host were scattered, out in the fields where the barley stood high and ready for the cutting and the grain was as golden as the sun was hot. A good harvest, as all had hoped, for it had been a bad year earlier with the cold, and there had been scant gleanings from a too-wet summer last year. Men had gone with empty bellies through the last of that cold and had sown grain they would joyfully have crammed by fistfuls into their mouths and chewed raw, even as they threw it into the waiting earth.

Not only in Britain had hunger pinched, but over-water, too. So that all men knew the winged-helmed invaders were on the prowl, and a coast watch had to be kept even though the men were needed in the fields.

Artos smeared the back of his hand across his forehead and tried not to wince as he straightened his aching back. Field work was harder than the training in the war band, though he had not had too much of that yet, just enough to prove how much he had yet to learn. He glanced now to where his shield mates were strung out in a straggling line along the field. It did not matter if one's father was Marius, troop commander under the Dragon himself. A man was matched against his own deeds, not by what his father, or his father's father, had done before him.

Artos had been named for the High King, Caesar of Britain, but he took his turn in the fields all the same. Just as he suffered the hard knocks of the wooden training sword when he was awkward or unlucky, or stupid enough not to be able to defend himself against Drusus' attack. Drusus was old now, but he could remember seeing the last of the Legions go down to the sea, taking the might of Rome with them, leaving Britain open to the sea wolves.

The High King had ridden north five days ago, to visit the posts manned against the Scots and the painted men in the north. And he had taken most of the Companions with him. Modred ruled here in Venta.

Artos scowled and kicked at a clod so that it crumbled under the toe of his boot. It was the High King (though Father always called him Caesar) who held Britain together. He had been just an army officer at first, but he had been loyal to Aurelianus, whom the real Caesar overseas had made Count of Britain. They had called Artos "Pendragon" and "Dux Bellorum" (Commander of Battles). Artos shaped the words though he did not speak them aloud; they had a ring to them. Men did not speak the true Latin of the empire any more, but added British words to everyday speech. Marius, like the High King, believed they should remember the past, and one way of doing that was to keep the language of men who had lived in cities and known the old lost days of peace.

For years now life had been only fighting. Men kept swords ever to hand, listened always for the roar of war horns. It was do that, live armed, or die under a Saxon ax—or worse, live a Saxon slave. The cities the Romans had built were mostly destroyed. Saxons hated cities and, when they could, reduced them to ruins. But Venta was where a Roman governor had once lived, and there were hill forts from the old days, which the King's men had rebuilt, forts which had once sheltered men from attack long before the coming of the Roman Legions.

Modred did not believe in keeping to the old ways. He smiled sneeringly behind backs—yes, and even to the faces of such as Marius and others of Caesar's men who wore short hair, went shaved of cheek and chin, carried the old Roman shields and armor. His men said openly now that it was better to forget Rome, to make peace with the Winged Helms, maybe even to give them some coast lands and swear blood-brother oaths with them, rather than fight forever.

Modred spoke only the British tongue, pretended not to understand Latin. He feasted the petty kings and chieftains of the north and the tribes. Marius, and the others like him, watched Modred with care. But many of the younger men treated Modred with deference, listened to him.

Artos bent back to his work. He hated the field more with every hour he was forced to spend in it. Why could he not have ridden north with Caesar's guard, with his father? He swung the harvest knife as if it were a sword, cutting the stalks raggedly. The furrows were endless and the sun hot, the day long.

One of the house slaves brought around the leather bottle of vinegar and water, and Artos drank his share. It was then that he saw the riders on the sea road. Their vividly colored cloaks were bright, thrown well back on their shoulders; in this heat they must be wearing them only for show. There was no mistaking Prince Modred as their leader.

Artos watched as they passed. But he was startled to see what the Prince wore about his arm just below the edge of his summer tunic's short sleeve. He would take oath that it was the Dragon armlet of the High King! But only Caesar, Artos Pendragon, had a right to that, and he had worn it himself when he had ridden out of Venta.

And Modred was not even the High King's heir by right, though men whispered that by some chance in the past he was truly the King's own son. But he was unlike Caesar in every way.

For Artos Pendragon was as tall as one of the forest trees, or so he looked among lesser men. And his hair, though he was now nigh an old man, was still the color of that rich gold which comes from the Western Isle. He wore his hair short and he shaved as did the Romans, which made him look younger than his years.

Whereas Modred was a good handsbreadth or more shorter, and dark of hair, the locks curling to his shoulders. Also he had wings of mustache curving on either side of his thin-lipped mouth, so that he looked as any of the tribal kings. He wore also their brightly colored clothes, cloaks woven in checkered patterns of green, red, and yellow, with like tunics and breeches, wide belts of soft leather studded with gold, a jeweled dagger, and a long sword.

Artos watched the party move on until they were hidden in the dust cloud. He longed to be ahorse and riding with them. No man could deny that Modred was a good fighter, and now he had been chosen by Caesar himself to hold Venta. He commanded all the forces except the Companions, who remained here, and the school for their sons, both of which were under the orders of Kai.

At the thought of Kai, Artos bent to work again, his shoulders hunching as if he already felt the sting of a willow switch laid smartly across them. Kai was a fighter, one of whom Marius thoroughly approved. You never won more than a grunt of half-satisfaction from Kai. But a grunt from that battle-scarred warrior was perhaps equal to half a Roman Triumph. Artos grinned. But still he remembered that armlet shining on Modred's darkly tanned arm and it cast a small seed of uneasiness into his mind.

It was his turn that night to wait upon the high table, bring in the drinking horns, set out the spoons and table knives. Modred's chair remained empty, as did two others, those of his close officers. Only Kai and Archais (who had come from overseas and was much learned in the healing of wounds) and Paulus, the priest, were there.

Artos listened to their talk, but there was little new to hear. Paulus was old and thought of little but the

Church, and he disliked Archais, as he made very plain, because the healer did not believe what Paulus taught. But this the priest could not say openly, because the High King had long since made it plain that what god a man chose to serve privately was his own business. This made the priests angry and they muttered a great deal, though there was naught they could do. However, lately they had been very bold about the need for peace, and Modred had those among them who talked so—too much, Marius said.

When the thin beer of the past year had been poured and the platters taken from the table, Archais spoke: "Our Lord Modred rides so far abroad that he cannot return for the evening meal?"

Kai shrugged. "That is his affair," he replied shortly. But the tone in his voice made Artos listen closely.

"The Winged Helms have been reported offshore. That fisherman from Deepdene reported sighting at least ten ships. It must be a raider with reputation to bring such a fleet. One thinks of Thorkiel—"

"No, no." Paulus shook his head. "Thorkiel would not dare. Did not our Lord King give him so grievous a beating yesteryear as to send him in fast flight?"

"These Winged Helms," growled Kai, "are like ants, Father. One can stamp out a scurry of them here, another there, yet there are always ants, and no end to them! They are only quiet when they are dead, but that takes a deal of doing. Good fighters they are, with their berserkers and their shield walls. Our Lord King knows the way to deal with them. Men sometimes laughed straight to his face in the beginning. But he went ahead with it, by Aurelianus' favor. He got horses, big ones—mostly before that we had just ponies, nothing to mount a grown man. And he found how to make armor for them and for their riders. He did not gather a big army such as

121

is hard to feed and easy to ambush—even the Legions learned that there were newer and better ways of fighting, good as they had been in their time.

"No, he took the horse companies and he was here, there, riding hard. We were so much in the saddle in those days that we got hard skin on our bottoms like calluses on the hands. And where the Saxons came, there we were—before they could expect it. Yes, the horse and the Companions cleared the land and kept it cleared.

"I remember the day they brought him the Dragon banner. It was new, a queer strange thing. Let the wind catch it rightly and it snapped out like a great red worm, its claws reaching for you. With that over a man's head, he got heart in him. Yes, we had the Dragon—'til it was cut to pieces. Seeing it seemed to send the heathen wild, and they would aim spears at it every time. But we just got us another, and another—all made the same. When the war horns call, the Dragon answers them!"

Artos knew the banner. There was a small one like it that flew from the watchtower of Venta when the High King was here and was carried with him when he traveled. But the big Dragon was kept safe until needed for battle. They called Caesar "Pendragon"—even just Dragon. And some of the people who did not know much actually thought he had a real dragon to help him in battle.

"But for all your valiant efforts, still these Winged Helms come," Archais observed.

"They come and they die." Kai pushed away from the table. "Always they come—it is a way of life."

"But need it be?" Paulus' voice sounded thin, almost like a whisper after Kai's deep-chested tones. "There is a way to keep peace and all men living in fellowship."

Kai laughed. "Cry 'pax' to a Winged Helm who has just beaten in your door, Father—one who has his ax ready to cut you down. There is only one *pax* for such."

His head swung to Artos, who had been very still and thought he was forgotten. "Youngling, get to your bed. Before cock's crow you'll be needed in the field again. With luck we'll be able to get in the rest of the barley before nightfall."

"With God's grace," Paulus corrected him. But Kai paid no attention to the priest as he stretched wide his hard-muscled arms.

Only, Artos was never to work in that barley field again. And it all came about because of the need for a drink of water.

He was tired enough to sleep soundly, but he roused out of a confused dream which afterward he could never remember; only, it left him feeling afraid. He sat up on the pallet which was his bed, feeling thirsty. Around him was the heavy, even breathing of the other sleepers. A thin sliver of moonlight shone in the hall without.

Once this maze of rooms, hallways, courtyards, had been the home and headquarters of a Roman governor. Now it was a rather badly kept palace, which few living within had ever totally explored.

The nearest water was in the great hall and Artos debated going after it. He ran a dry tongue over cracked lips and thought that he must. He had worn his breeches and leggings to bed, he had been so tired, and he did not wait now to pick up his tunic as he padded across the chamber, careful to avoid the pallets of the others.

In the hall the moonlight came through the window. There was another source of light, too, a dim glow in another chamber. Artos was curious. Who could be there? It was well away from any place where the guard were on watch duty. That curiosity sent him to see, creeping up with caution toward the half-open door.

He passed the shut door of Kai's chamber. Beyond it were two empty rooms, usually occupied by men who were now riding north with the King. That left only the arms room. But why—?

Artos edged his way along, close to the wall. He could hear a very faint murmur of voices, sounds of men moving about. He reached the place where the door swung out, shielded himself behind it to peer through the crack.

Modred—there was no mistaking the young man who sat at the table where the armorer kept his supply lists. But beyond him were three men wearing the scale armor of the Companions—young men. Artos knew two of them by name as clansmen who had been recruited a couple of years ago. The third was Argwain, who prided himself on being blood-kin of Modred through one of the complicated clan reckonings.

Artos could not believe what he saw. They had opened the dragon chest. Its lock was broken—Kai had the keeping of the key. And now they were pulling out the coils of the Red Dragon, folding the banner with more haste than care, to cram into a bag Argwain held ready. Torchlight glinted on Modred's arm as he changed position. Artos saw his guess proven true. That was a king's royal arm ring, twin to the one Caesar wore.

The Dragon, the armlet, Modred— How those fitted together the boy did not know. But there was evil here, like black smoke curling from a fire.

"—to the west. Show him this and bid him land where the four torches move right to left before full moonrise." Modred was speaking.

"You." The Prince turned then to Argwain. "Take the signal to Maegwin, to Caldor. We shall so cut the land apart before they can drag themselves out of their fields and take up sword to front us. And with that"—he nodded to the bagged Dragon banner—"and such news as we can proclaim, there will be few swords left to them.

Men shall not be sure what is true or false until it is too late!"

"No man can say that you do not plan well, Lord King," Argwain nodded.

"This has been long in planning, but now we act. Let us go."

Artos had only time to push away from the door, dodge into one of those empty rooms. He stood in the gloom within, his heart pounding, rubbing sweating palms against his breeches, trying to make sense of what he had heard.

Modred had the armlet and the banner, and Argwain had called him king. He spoke of torches to signal a landing. And this talk of peace-making with the Winged Helms—their ships reported offshore— All made so ugly a pattern that Artos could not believe it added up as he feared. He must tell Kai!

The men were surely gone from the arms room now. He crossed the hall to the closed door of the commander's chamber, pushing it open only wide enough for him to slip through. The moon shone through a window to show a low bedstead, and he could hear the rumbling snore of the sleeper who lay there. Artos laid a hand on the man's bare shoulder.

Kai had the warrior's trick of waking instantly, his wits alert, and as he raised himself on his elbows Artos crouched by the bed, spilling out what he had seen and heard. There was a muffled exclamation from Kai, and he sat fully up, his feet meeting the floor with a thud.

"What this may mean," he said, "is not to be judged hastily. But that the High King must know goes without arguing." He rubbed fist against fist, and in the moonlight Artos could see the scowl on his face.

"Listen, you," he spoke then directly to the boy. "This must not be done openly. A known messenger riding forth would give away that they had been discovered, if he were not also followed and cut down."

"I ride light and I ride as Marius taught," Artos dared to say.

"Ay, and the High King lies at the hill camp near Fenters Hold. The Roman Way runs north to the Wall, and it is cut by a traders' track to the sea. It is a clear way."

"And I have ridden part of it," Artos was proud to say. "I went to the Wall two summers ago when my father held truce meeting with the Painted People."

"So you did. Which is another piece of fortune." Kai pulled at his thumb, turning the circlet there around and around to free it from its long grip on his flesh. It was a giant's ring to look at, broad and heavy, with a queerly shaped red stone showing the head of a man with horns. Paulus said it was evil, but Kai said that it had belonged to his father, and *his* father, and that it had come overseas in the far-off days, before the Legions set foot in Britain.

He worked it free with an effort. "This is known, boy. Do not take any horse from the stable here, you would be marked and questioned. Slip into town and on to the post of the first hill watch. They keep messenger mounts. Show this and take the road north. Change at any hill fort when your beast begins to fail. For it is time which draws sword against us in this matter. Now—let us go."

Artos slipped from shadow to shadow across the streets of Venta. He wore a tunic and cloak now, as well as his own sword belted heavy against him. Marius had traded for that sword two years ago at the meeting with the Painted People. It was a Legion sword, Marius said, loot from some long-ago battle along the Wall perhaps. But the blade was good and Artos' father had haggled for a long time to get it. It was shorter than the swords the Companions favored, but it was just right for Artos. He had a pouch of rations, too. And Kai's ring was slung on a thong around his neck for safekeeping.

He might have been questioned if he had not had the ring to show when he reached the hill watch. The horse they brought him—stripped to a light saddle pad for speed—though undersize in comparison to the chargers of the Companions, was picked, he knew, for the steady, mile-eating pace it could keep. And he pounded off along the road, thankful for the smooth pavement the Legion had built.

The road ran due north, and though more years than Artos was old had passed since it had been repaired, it was still good footing. Sun rose, and midmorn came. He changed mounts at another of the hill forts. The men here were from one of the tribes, as their plaid tunics made plain. They rained questions upon Artos as he leaned against the log wall, gulping down mouthfuls of bread with just enough barley beer to make it swallowable. To all he only shook his head and said he was on the High King's business and the message he carried was not of his understanding.

Once more, after noon, when the sun was hot and he had to fight against nodding in the saddle, he changed mounts. This time the watchers were in a crumbling Roman tower. They wore no armor, nor even the brilliant dress of the tribes, but rather had tanned hides on their small, dark bodies marked with blue tattoos. They had bows and arrows, and they spoke in a soft, clipped speech to one another. But their leader—who had a cloak of wolf skin in spite of the heat, the wolf's head with its upper jaw resting on the man's head, dozens of ivory fangs necklaced about his throat—spoke Latin, though in a strange singsong.

Though Artos had never seen these people so closely

before, he knew them to be Picts from over the Wall—who served not the land of Britain but rather one man alone, the High King. For Artos Pendragon had in some way won their favor and they came to his call.

Tribesmen, Picts, and a small handful of men who, like Marius, still called themselves "Roman" with harsh pride —these made up the High King's army. Among themselves they would have been sword against sword, knife against arrow. But under Artos Pendragon they were one. His greatest gift was that he could make a victorious army out of such normally divided forces.

Soon after he left the watchtower, Artos swung into the west way. Here he had to slacken pace, since this was no paved road but a wandering tract which turned and twisted with rough footing. There were no grain fields to be seen and here the King's peace was more often broken than kept.

The moon was once more up when the boy saw the scarlet leap of campfires. He slid from his mount, so stiff he could only walk with his hand laid in support against the shoulder of the stumbling horse. His throat was dry with dust as he croaked an answer to the sentry. And he was never quite sure how he came into the High King's chamber.

"It is young Artos! But what do you here? Call Marius."

"Lord King." This time Artos managed better than the croak, found a horn pushed into his hand, and drank some of the bitter beer before he went on. "Lord King"— he fumbled for Kai's ring—"Legatus Kai has sent me."

"To come in such a plight smells of trouble. What manner? Do the Winged Helms— But then the alarm torches would have flamed across country to warn us long since. What is it?"

Then those big, strong hands lay gently on his

shoulders, drawing him closer, supporting him. Artos spilled out word after word of what he had seen and heard. There were confused voices about him, but they meant little. Then, somehow, he was lying on a camp pallet, and his father's dark, clean-shaven face, surmounted by a plumed helm, was close to his. He knew he had done what he had come to do.

So the dark time began, and afterward Artos sometimes wondered what might have happened had some small chance led them in a different way.

He was not the only messenger Kai sent, but his forewarning gave the High King some precious hours, which he used well. Other riders went out with the warn-call. Harvest time—Modred had chosen the time for his treachery well.

As men straggled in, a handful here, a better-disciplined war band there, they learned that Modred had indeed raised the Red Dragon and taken a blood oath with the Winged Helms. Ten ships had the fisherman reported off the coast, but now came tales of twenty, more at sea edging in. It would be such a bloodletting to come as would crush all the High King had fought for, unless he could hold the invaders to the coast.

"But Modred is mad—!" Artos, now his father's trumpeter, watched Marius bring his bronzed fist down upon the table, setting the drinking horns shaking with the force of his blow.

"No, far from mad," the High King replied. "Remember Vortigen? Modred is of his line, and so sees himself more truly King of Britain than I. By the reasoning of half the tribes I have no right to this." His hand twitched forward a fold of the purple cloak draped across the back of his seat. "Until Aurelianus gave me power I was no more than a man with a plan and a dream. Though now that seems long ago. However"—

now he spoke more briskly—"no matter how royal Modred deems himself and is hailed by those deluded enough to believe that this time they can play Vortigen's game with the Saxons and win, I am not about to let the axes of the Winged Helms bring down what is left of life and light in this land.

"Therefore—" He began to talk briskly of men and the movements of an army, those about him listening carefully. Artos saw his father nod once or twice, heard an assenting grunt from Gawain, who ordered the left wing when the Companions charged.

In the end the High King made a small gesture and the serving men hastened to fill the drinking horns, not with the usual thin beer but rather with the strong-smelling mead of the northlands. Then did Artos Pendragon raise his horn high, get to his feet, the others scrambling up to join him.

"Comrades, it may be that this time we go into dark ways. But if that be so I will say it now—we cannot go in better company! If Modred would buy the kingship, and the Winged Helms this land, then let the price be high!"

There was an answering growl as men drank and threw the horns from them, to roll empty across the table.

When Artos and his father went back to their own quarters, Marius stood for a moment eying his son.

"I would have you ride now to Glendower."

"No!" For the first time in his life Artos found the courage to say that to his father, and in spite of the other's deepening frown he hurried on. "Is this army so great a single sword can be spared?"

"A boy's sword? You are no man to ride—"

"And if—if Modred's men come to Glendower? What of our neighbor Iscar? He has long wanted our lands.

130

You can send me forth only bound and gagged and under guard!"

Marius must have read his son's determination, for suddenly he looked very tired and gave a small shrug. "So be it. But if you stay you are under my orders."

Artos drew a deep breath. "That I know."

Thus he was one of the army that marched south and west. Army? It was hardly a full troop to begin with, though men continued to gather and add to the number as they went. More messengers arrived with ill news of the Saxons pushing inland and of Modred setting up a camp to which came men of the tribes, swearing blood oaths of loyalty under the stolen Red Dragon.

The High King laughed harshly when he was told of this.

"Blood oaths, is it? Do they remember that in the past such oaths were also given to me?"

"But the priests say that they are absolved of them, since they were given to one who did not hold the true church in reverence," observed Gawain with a twist of lip. It was well known that he was one who followed the old gods, and that the High King had many times been urged by the priests to turn him away for that very reason.

"Men cannot be absolved from treachery so easily," was all that Pendragon answered.

But it seemed that traitor or not, Modred was gathering the greater host. And only half of it marched under the horse-tail standards of the Saxons.

Artos rode as Marius' trumpeter and messenger, always at his father's back as he cantered alone at the head of the troop. Most of them were of the old Roman breed. They used the shorter swords of the Legions, and their faces, overshadowed by the old crested helms, differed from those of the tribesmen. Their standard was an Eagle, mounted on a pole, its wings outspread.

Caius carried it, and his place, too, was behind his commander. Artos envied him that honor. The war horn bumping at his own hip was not nearly as fine a symbol as that Eagle.

There came a time when at last they could see the fires of the enemy camp. But between lay a swampy, broken land, unfit for horses.

"Modred has chosen well," Artos heard his father say to the first Centurion, Remus, as they looked down from a hillock.

"Traitor though he be, he is still a fighting man. But then he has not yet met Caesar in battle." There was confidence in Remus' answer.

They had further additions to their force. Kai came out of Venta with what was left of the defenders there. Artos saw among them a sprinkling of his in-training comrades, so the old and the very young had closed ranks together. Yet no Red Dragon led the van now.

The High King would not let them use the pinion symbolic of his rulership. Instead he gave orders that each man break a handful of barley in stalk from the fields as he marched (so many fields were left without reapers now) and bind it to his helm in sign that he fought not for any king's honor but for his own land. So it was that a large tuft was on the haft of a spear carried behind the High King as he rode, and a twist about the Eagle carried by Caius.

That night came a sounding of horns for parley across the broken land, now well lighted by torches. Then came a band not of fighting men but of priests, craving speech with the King. They were led by Imfry, one of those who had argued in the past with Pendragon because he would not give more power to the church. Yet the High King had ever treated him with courtesy.

Of that meeting Artos heard only what his father told later—that the churchmen urged a truce wherein Modred and the High King might meet face to face, and perhaps the land escape a bath of blood.

"What of the Saxons?" Artos asked.

Marius laughed harshly. "Ay, the Saxons. But the priests are ever hopeful for the winning of their souls. Their leader, Bareblade, has listened to Imfry, it seems. Well, Caesar will grant them their truce meeting. That will gain us more time, which is our greatest need. There is no trusting in the promises of either Modred or Saxon. Each is to bring an armed following of ten, but with strict orders not to draw blade for any reason. To show steel is to break peace."

"Do you go?" To Artos' relief Marius shook his head.

"Caesar takes only two of his captains, Kai and Gawain. If it be a trap he must not lose all of us. And meanwhile, truce or no, we shall be battle-mounted when they go."

The sun was well up when the High King and his selected followers rode out from the lines of his war host. From those other ranks, where the horse tails of the Winged Helms were insolently planted and the Dragon shaft stood, came others.

"Their Dragon sulks," Caius murmured to Artos.

That was true enough. The red banner was not proudly bellied out in the wind but hung limp as a tattered rag about its standard. Perhaps it was an omen that the banner of the High King would come to life for him alone.

As the two parties met, the priests to one side chanted a hymn, which reached the watchers as a faint murmur of sound. The sun grew hotter as they waited. Now and then someone in the company spoke in a low voice to his neighbor. But the stamp of a horse because of the flies, the grate of armor as someone shifted position, broke the silence more noticeably.

The ground before them was heath, bog in some patches, ill footing for mounted men. There were some scattered clumps of stunted firs, but mostly coarse grass, sun-browned until it was near the color of ripe grain.

Artos saw a flash of light. One of Modred's men had drawn sword, was stabbing down at the ground. His steel was bare.

"Truce broke! Truce broke!" The cry began low, but swelled into a roar as man after man took it up.

Below was a tangle of men, swords out, clashing—

"Sound!"

Artos did not need that order, the war horn was already at his lips. Its harsh call was lost among other sounds. And then began the charge the High King had planned, the men of the company shouting "Ave, Caesar!" as they rode.

The rest of it was a madness which Artos could never remember except in small snatches. For he was swallowed up in it, swinging the Roman sword. There were distorted faces which came into view and vanished, then once or twice a breathing space when the men of the troop came together and re-formed, to be sent to charge again.

Artos saw Caius go down under a Saxon ax and grabbed the Eagle before it was lost, using its pole to drive against the head of the man who had killed its bearer, knocking him from his feet so that the horses went over him. Each time the troop re-formed the lines were thinner, more men in them were wounded, some clinging to their saddles only by force of will.

The sky darkened, but yet there was light enough to see about them. The High King, his Caesar's purple cloak a ragged fringe; his shield, its garnet-eyed dragon's head half shorn away, still on his arm; and that great sword about which there were such awesome tales, red in his hand—the High King, Artos of Britain!

Fronting him was Prince Modred, all his royal finery spoiled by this day's foul work.

"No!" The Prince's voice rose in a great cry, as if to see that the King still lived was more than he could bear. He rushed forward, his sword ready. The King prepared to meet his charge.

Modred struck first at the horse and it reared screaming, while the Prince dodged those flailing hoofs. Artos Pendragon came out of the saddle, but he landed badly, stumbling, so that Modred, low like a serpent, thrust around his shield. His blade caught on the rent rim and he could not withdraw it quickly for a second stroke. The High King struck in return, a mighty blow across the other's body where neck met shoulder. Modred staggered to one side, dead before his body crumpled to the ground.

But the High King wavered on a pace or two, until one of the kicking legs of his dying horse hit him and he, too, fell.

"Ahhhh"—a moan came from the bloodied and battered men near the King. Artos lurched out of the saddle, tottered on to pull at the High King, trying to drag him away from the horse, others elbowed him aside, unheeding of the enemy, to free their leader.

Then a shout warned them and they looked up to see Saxons running toward them. They fought a wild, desperate battle around Pendragon. And so great was their grief and rage that they paid no heed to wounds. But as if they were men of iron, who could take no hurt, they cut down the Winged Helms.

When that swirl of battle had subsided there remained

only five of the Companions still on their feet. Artos crouched beside the King where he had tried to shield that body with the hacked and splintered pole of the Eagle and his own flesh. The standard was shorn of a wing and blood ran warm from his arm. His fingers were numb, unable longer to grasp a sword hilt.

The King stirred and moaned. Somehow they got him out of the press of the dead, to where he could lie straight on the ground. Artos looked around, dazed. Kai lay, his sword deep in a Saxon, but his own craggy face empty of life. Marius? Where was his father? One of those bending over the fallen king looked up.

"Artos?"

The boy could not answer aloud. Using the staff of the Eagle as a support, he hobbled to where the King lay with those others gathered around him. It was Marius who said, "This is a grievous wound, but we must get him into hiding. There is no way yet of telling how this day has gone. And they would rejoice greatly to set his head on one of their spears."

Among them they carried him away. It was hard labor, for he was a large and heavy man and they were all spent, no man without some wound. Artos stumbled along in their wake, still leaning on his pole. But as he circled to the left to avoid a tangle of dead men and horses he came upon the Royal Standard. The pole had been planted firmly in the earth. About it the Red Dragon hung limp and lifeless, as if it would serve none but its true master. Artos could hardly see it in the twilight. He pushed the broken end of the Eagle shaft into the ground to keep it upright and pulled at the Dragon's pole. It had been too firmly set to yield to his weak tugging. At last he went to his knees and dug in the earth with his belt knife until he could pull it free.

It was heavy and he had to rest it across his good

shoulder. The folds, smelling of wood smoke, draped about his head. But he brought it with him, trailing those who carried the King.

They found a rough little hut, perhaps the shelter of some holy man who had chosen to dwell in the wilderness alone, as some did nowadays. Someone had kindled a fire, and by its light they were easing off the King's armor to examine his wound.

No man with the true healing knowledge was there. But they had been long enough at war to know the look of hurts men could take. Marius sat back on his heels, his face a dark mask. Artos turned away his eyes.

"Marius?"

"Caesar!" He bent again over his lord.

"This is my death hurt—"

"I have seen men take worse and live."

"Use such words for a child, Marius. This is the dark road after all. But truss me up as best you can. I shall hold to life until I know—know how it fares with Britain. Let me know how went the day—"

"Be sure you shall!" Marius turned to the others, all wounded. "Sextus, Calyn, Gondor—see what you can learn!"

They were the least hurt of that company and they went swiftly.

"At least that traitor Modred is dead!" Marius spat.

"All deeds—bring—their—own—reward," the High King said. "Is—there—aught—to drink?"

"There is a mere beyond." Marius got to his feet. "It is doubtless scummed, but it is still water." He pulled off his helmet, crestless where its plume had been cut away, and went out. Artos leaned the heavy pole of the banner against the wall, slipped down to sit with his back against the rough surface. His wound had stopped bleeding, but his arm was still numb.

It was a long night, but the King spoke now and then. Sometimes Artos could hear his words clearly, sometimes they were only a murmur, faint and faraway. Marius tended his son's wound and bound it with a strip torn from his cloak, ordering him to sleep if he could.

Men came, to glance within the hut and look upon the King. Some he greeted by name, one or two came to kneel beside him for a space. But they all remained without as a guard about the hut. Slowly news came, too. Modred's forces had melted away when the story of the Prince's death reached them. The Saxons had been driven back to the shore by fresh troops come too late for the real battle. But the war host that had followed the Caesar of Britian, the Companions of the Red Dragon, had been so rent and destroyed that it could never ride as an army again.

When the dawn came, and with it the news that the Saxon host was taking to ship under the harrying of the new levies, the High King listened greedily. Then he turned to Marius and spoke, his voice a little stronger, as if he had been hoarding his strength against this time.

"I made the war host, and now it is broken. But my name may hold men together yet awhile so you can gain time. A dream it was, a good dream—of a Britain united against the dark night of the heathen. We made it live, if only for a space, but now it dies. Do the best you can, Gawain, Marius, those like you, to remember the dream in the coming night. Now, that I may serve dead even as I served living, do not let any save those in this hut known that I die. But say rather that I go to be healed, that my wound, though it be deep, is not fatal.

"We are not far from the river. Get a boat, if you can, and lay me on some island there, making sure that there be no marking of my grave. Swear this to me as the last loyal oath I ask of you."

And together they swore. He did not speak again, but a little later Marius, leaning over him, laid hand on the King's forehead, rose, and nodded. Then he came swiftly to the great Dragon banner and slashed at the cords which bound it to the pole, cutting it also as it lay flat upon the ground. Into it they laid the High King. When they carried him forth they said to the waiting guard that they would take him now to the holy men who lived downriver, who knew the healing arts.

Marius and Gawain found a boat and put the King in it, Artos crept behind his father. Sextus rowed and the boat answered well. Then they were caught in the current and let it bear them along. At last they came to an island covered with brush and small trees, some of them bearing small, half-ripe apples. Who had planted them in this wilderness, Artos could not guess.

Breaking through the barrier of reeds and brush, Marius, Bawain, and Sextus carrying the King, they came to an open space in which stood a small building of rough stone. The carven statue of a woman was just within its portal, two others, though smaller, standing a little behind her. That it was a temple of the old days Artos guessed, but honoring what goddesses, British or Roman, he did not know.

There before the temple, with the three statues seeming to watch, they dug into the earth with their swords. Marius' blade broke against a stone he was trying to lever away. He reached within the roll of the Dragon banner and drew forth the King's longer and heavier weapon, to hack at the clay. Meanwhile Artos pushed away the loosened soil the others tossed out of that cutting.

It took them a long time, for the swords were unhandy spades, and Marius and the others sought to make the hole a deep one. Then they pulled fresh reeds from the shore, and leaves, which, when crushed in their soil-grimed hands, gave forth clean smells. Artos found a bed of small flowers by the temple and jerked them up. From these they made the bed of him who was the last Caesar of Britain. Then, well wrapped in his war banner, Artos Pendragon, the High King, was laid in his hidden grave.

They worked long once more to fill in and cover the place. When they had done and were ready to go, Artos suddenly saw the King's sword lying where his father had dropped it. That should have been buried, too, in the hand of its owner.

He held it out to his father in mute question. Marius took it with a sigh, ran his hand along the scarred, notched blade.

"It is too well known. So it must also disappear. For no man would believe that Caesar would willingly let it go from him."

He went down to the river bank and whirled it above his head with all the force left in his tired arms, letting it fly out over the water and splash into the dark flood. So it was gone, the last tie they had with Artos Pendragon, Dux Bellorum, Caesar, High King of Britain. And the sun went down.

5

SHUI MIEN LUNG— SLUMBERING DRAGON

Artie rubbed his eyes with one hand. They smarted with tears, his cheeks were also wet. But there was no river, no trees, no temple with three goddesses left to watch over a hidden grave. He blinked and blinked again. He was not Artos—but Artie, Artie Jones. And he was sitting in a chair beside a table. A beam of sun shone straight on the bright red dragon he had pieced together, joined with the silver and the blue ones. It was the dragon of the banner, the one in which they had wrapped *him*. Artie smeared his hand across his face again and sniffed hard.

He was *crying!* Like a little kid! But—the dream—it had been so real! He felt as if he were still on that shore ready to get into the boat, to go back to the camp of what was left of the army. What had happened after-ward?

King Arthur—they had read about King Arthur in school. But those had been stories about knights, and the Round table, and—not like this Arthur at all! He wanted to know what did happen to Artos, Marius, the rest. Did anyone ever discover that the High King was dead? Or did they keep on fighting and hoping that he would come back to lead them? Something in Artie was firm in the belief that it had really happened, all of it—the treachery of Modred, the death of Pendragon, the secret burial.

When he thought of Modred he felt somehow a little ashamed, not of the Prince but of himself. Artos had envied Modred's men, wanted a little to be a part of that war band, but Modred had been ready to throw away all Pendragon had fought for just that he might be himself king.

Artie frowned—he was thinking about Modred and Artos—sometimes it was easy to choose the wrong side—just because you wanted to be a part of something which showed—showed—he wasn't quite sure yet how that would work out. But now most of all he knew it had all happened once.

He slipped off the chair and his foot touched the football. It rolled out into the hall. Artie hurried after it. He did not look again at the red dragon (he did not have to, he would remember it always). Picking up the ball, he retraced his way through the house.

Not until he was in the overgrown garden did Artie think of something else. Those other two dragons that had been put together—did they have stories, too? Was that why Sig and Ras had gone there? Maybe they knew more about Artos—what had happened to him! Artie started on at a trot. He would hunt up the two boys, find out what they knew.

He slowed as he came to Sig's house, half hoping he might see the other boy. But there was no sign of him. Reluctantly Artie moved on. Tomorrow they were going to the Grands' for dinner, no chance to see Sig. Monday morning, though, at the bus stop—if he got there a little early and Sig did too, maybe he could hint around and find out whether Sig had had any adventure with the other dragons. He wanted to know so badly!

Never had a weekend passed so slowly for Artie. He ran into trouble several times when he was thinking about Pendragon and the rest. People asked him questions and he did not answer. He was glad when Sunday night came and they were back home. He went to his room, saying he had homework (he even tried to work some problems in math, read some history). Only, there kept coming between him and the pages little parts of the dream. He could feel again the pain in his arm as he watched Marius and the others hacking at the earth with their swords.

Artie sighed. One thing he wanted to do was to find out more about Arthur—his Arthur, not the fairy-tale one. There might be a book at the library. Artie did not know much about the library. He went there when he had to get a book for a report, but then he just hunted for the thinnest one he could find. Greg Ross's crowd had a list of thin books they passed around, he had seen them doing it.

Greg Ross—with surprise Artie realized that this was the first time since Saturday he had thought about Greg. Somehow not being noticed by Greg's crowd did not matter any more. What did Greg Ross mean to someone who had been trusted by Kai, who had gone in battle, who had—Once more Artie relived the exciting parts of his dream. Greg Ross dwindled pretty small when he thought about him now. It was much more important to see Sig tomorrow.

There was only one big boy at the bus stop the next morning—Kim Stevens. Sighting him, disappointed, Artie slowed to a stop and looked the other way. Kim was reading again, a book close to his nose. He was always reading. Maybe that's why he had to wear glasses, he read so much. And he did not look up or say anything as Artie took a stand to watch down the street for Sig.

But when Sig swung into view he had Ras with him. Artie hesitated. Though he wanted to talk to Sig, he knew that both Sig and Ras had been in that house fussing around with the puzzle. So, drawing on his courage, Artie stepped deliberately out in their path.

"Hi," he said, but that greeting did not come out as confidently as he meant it to; rather, it was more as if he were afraid they were not going to answer him.

Sig stared at him for a moment and Ras scowled. Artie was ready to call it quits, only his desperate need to know brought out a rush of words. "Please, you guys, about those dragons—" He had not meant to go at it just like that, the words seemed to say themselves.

Now they were looking at him as if they did want to hear what he had to say.

"What dragons?" Ras demanded.

"The silver one—the blue one—"

Sig grabbed Artie by the arm. "What have you been doing? Snooping around?"

"Wait!" Ras set a shoulder between Sig and Artie. He was watching Artie intently.

"Which one did you make?" he asked in a low voice, hardly above a whisper.

Artie answered promptly with the truth. "The red one, Pendragon."

"Pendragon?" repeated Sig. He lessened the roughness of his hold on Artie, but he looked more to Ras as he asked, "You know Pendragon?"

"Pendragon? No, never heard of that before. But then I never heard of Fafnir or the lau before either. All right, Artie, so you put together the red dragon, this Pendragon. Then what happened? Give, man!"

Artie told in a bubble of words which got things rather mixed up so that his listeners kept interrupting him with questions he answered impatiently. But he told in detail of the burial of the High King, the throwing of his sword into the river.

"Did—did you dream about him, too?" he ended.

"Not him—" Sig was beginning when the bus came

and they climbed in, hurrying for the long seat at the back where they could crowd in together.

"I had Fafnir and Sigurd," Sig said under the hum of other voices. "And Ras had Sirrush-Lau and Daniel. Tell him, Ras."

Ras's story was much shortened, but he was able to make Artie believe in his adventure. They continued to compare notes, each adding more details of his particular dragon venture, sometimes talking all at once.

"There is still the yellow dragon," Sig said, "I wonder—"

Ras shook his head. "Won't do us any good to try, you know what happened before. But I sure would like to know what dragon that is. Not that we ever shall, now. The wreckers are coming this week and the Good Will people have to clean the house out. That puzzle will go with the rest of the stuff."

"I wish it could be finished. It ought to be!" Sig thumped his fist down on his big notebook. "I want to know what dragon that is."

The word "dragon" carried to the seat ahead. Although Kim was reading he could catch some of their conversation, just as he had also been aware of their excited words at the bus stop. Now he still held his book open, but instead of reading he listened with all his might to learn more.

Even the fact that the three, who had never paid any attention to one another before, were now so friendly was surprising. They apparently had become a tightly knit group. Dragons—he thought about dragons.

Kim knew a lot of dragon lore from China. There was the green dragon of the east; the dragons who rose to the sky in the spring and plunged into the waters in the fall; Lung, the five-toed dragon, who in the old days could be pictured only in the royal palace or on the robes of the Emperor; the heavenly dragons who guarded the mansions of the old gods; spirit dragons who controlled winds and rain; earth dragons who cleared rivers, deepened seas; the dragons who guarded hidden treasures.

Dragons could take on the bodies of men and appear if they wished among people. He knew the old tales about such dragons and the gifts they gave those they favored, the evil they could do in return to evil men. Yes, there were a lot of stories about dragons. But that's all they were—just stories. What did these three talking behind him now know about dragons? Now as much as he did. Not that they would ever listen to him. Suppose he turned around right now and said—

But that was the last thing he was going to do! Kim hated this bus ride, he hated this school! He wanted to go back to the old one, where he knew people. The book he held shook a little, but he continued to use it as a screen. At least, while he looked as if he were reading, no one was going to guess how lonely he was each day. Reading made a good cover to hide the fact that he had no one to talk to, anyway.

A book for a screen. Screens—the old people in China had used screens to shut out demons. Sometimes dragons were carved or pictured on them to frighten the demons. He wished he might summon up a real Chinese dragon— the best kind. What would people say if, like a Taoist sorcerer, he came riding to school on one?

Dragons—but how could there be dragons in that old house? Kim thought of the few words he had caught clearly, puzzled over them. An idea sprang into his mind. What if he went there himself to see? But one did not enter an empty house, it was against the law.

Only, this house was going to be torn down soon, maybe even this week. So it was not breaking and entering—or was it? A dragon—dragons—those boys mentioned more than one in the house. Pictures or carvings, or maybe a screen. He had heard that the man who once lived there had traveled all over the world. It could well be that he had brought dragon pictures back from the East. And Kim wanted to know—he had to know!

Kim noted that when the bus let them off at the school Artie made no move to hurry away to where Greg Ross and his friends stood arguing over Saturday's game. Rather, he stayed with Sig and the boy who called himself Ras, all three of them still talking excitedly together. Also, when they were able to ask for library passes in the homeroom period, Kim was not the only one who put up his hand. The three did the same for the first time he could remember.

He watched them in the library, as well as he could when he thought they would not guess that he was doing so. Sig and Ras appeared to know what they wanted. But Artie hesitated and then asked a question of the librarian. She seemed a little surprised and went to the catalog to turn over cards, leaving the drawer open a fraction when she went on to the shelves to pick out a book.

Kim went to the catalog, pulled out the drawer, and looked. There was an open space and he read the title of the book on the card at that point. *The Lantern Bearers,* a book about Roman Britain. He had read it at the other school. It was good—all about the time when the Legions had to leave Britain and the people were left to fight the Saxon invaders on their own. There was a lot in it about the man who was supposed to be the real King Arthur, not the one with the knights and the Round Table.

But what had that to do with dragons? And what were Sig and Ras so interested in? Completely mystified, Kim managed to stand in the checkout line just behind them, making an effort to see the books each held.

Sig had one of hero tales, Ras one on ancient Egypt.

Artie joined the line immediately behind Kim with his selection. As they started for the next class the three joined forces again, each showing his book to the others. But what did Egypt, hero stories, and Roman Britain have in common? Kim shoved his own absent-minded choice into his book bag, absorbed more and more by the mystery of this sudden alliance.

He thought about it off and on all day, until at last he made up his mind. The roots of the mystery must certainly lie in the old house, and it had something to do with dragons.

Much as he had held apart from the boys in this new school (they looked upon him as a—they called it "kook," as he had heard several times), this mystery made him suddenly want to actually solve it. Even if that meant trailing the three, or poking into what they would consider their business alone.

He would not have much time, perhaps no longer than today. So he would try after school, though he still felt queer about going in the old house. If the boys themselves went back he would go after them.

But the three did not even glance at the old house as they got off the bus that afternoon. Instead they went straight on up the street. Sig lived the closest. Kim followed very slowly, trying to make up his mind for sure. When they reached Sig's house they went along in with him, still talking.

Now Kim walked very slowly indeed. Sig's front door opened and banged shut. They were safe inside. What should he do? He had to make up his mind quickly, there would not be much time. Mother would wonder why he was not home if he lingered too long.

He made his decision and hurried back to the drive which led to the old house. Though he still had caution enough to pause there and make sure no one was watching. There were plenty of bushes, you could slip along behind those.

The front door had a big board nailed right across it. Where had Sig, the others, gone in? Must be around back somewhere. Kim plowed through the piles of leaves toward the rear of the house. He saw the porch and the muddy tracks across it, leading to the window. That was it. Again he paused. What was he going to do? He could still go back. Only, a second later he knew that he never could. He had to follow this adventure to the end.

Kim struggled to raise the window and then climbed in. Here was a big, dark room. He had been stupid to come without a flashlight. But to get one meant going home, and then maybe not being able to get back. There was light enough to see across the big kitchen, maybe enough in the rest of the house for him to explore. They had all been here before him. And if Artie and Sig and Ras could do it, so could Kim Stevens.

But he did take off his glasses and give them an extra polish with his handkerchief, as if that could make him see better through the gloom. There were odd noises, little creaks, sighs, which made him uneasy, though he knew that they must come from old boards, and maybe rats or mice, things you find in old houses where no one has lived for some time.

Kim pushed on through the pantry to the dining room, stopping to look about there. Nothing here to suggest even the smallest dragon. He thought the big old furniture was dull and ugly, and there was thick dust everywhere.

Nor did the living room, with all the furniture covered with sheets and newspapers, have anything in it to suggest that anyone had explored here. No dragon pictures or carvings, though Kim wiped the dust by hand from a couple of glass-fronted cabinets, to see within some cups and saucers and small figures of people and animals.

There was a hall beyond and here were tracks to guide him to the doorway of another room. The door was ajar and he paused to listen. Almost he expected to hear movement beyond. He had the strangest feeling, as if something stood on the other side waiting for him. But after a moment or two Kim knew it was not dangerous at all, only exciting.

He opened the door a little wider and slipped inside. There was nothing there but a table and a chair sitting by it, as if someone had just left. But light came from one uncovered window and on the table were colors, very bright colors, glowing almost like small lamps.

He went closer to those jewel-like colors. A puzzle! He had had one given to him last Christmas. It had been round, with all kinds of wild animals on it. They had all helped put it together. Mother had set up a table in the room just to hold it while they could work on it. And it had taken a long time to put it together, almost a week.

Kim picked up the lid of the box to look at the guide picture. Dragons! Four of them, all different. And three of them had been fitted together already. Only the golden one was still a spill of pieces on the tabletop. He examined the picture of it on the cover. It was an imperial dragon—the five-toed Lung! Now, as he looked at the other three, he saw that they were not Chinese—especially the strange blue one. But the gold one was just like those he had seen pictured so many times in Hong Kong.

A lot of the pieces on the table were upside-down and there were red markings on them, like the brush strokes of the old-time writing. Kim poked a few around with a fingertip, and of themselves almost they snapped together so that a red character was plain. He knew a few of the old characters—not many—he could not really read much. Though this one looked strange at first, it made sense.

Just one character, written in red. Another idea swam into his mind, though he did not know from where. In the old days the Emperor was always supposed to write in vermilion, and was not vermilion a kind of red color? Kim wondered where he had learned that.

This character—memory he was not sure of supplied a word, or rather two words: Shui Mien. That meant "sleeping." But how did he know that? He was sure he had never seen that character before.

Shui Mien—Lung, added his scrap of memory. Kim was startled, more than a little afraid. Shui Mien Lung! It was as if someone standing unseen in the dusty, half-dark room had repeated the words for him. Yet he had heard nothing—it was as if he heard it in his *mind!* If you could *hear* with your *mind!*

Shui Mien Lung—sleeping dragon. No, again that strange mind-voice corrected him: "Slumbering dragon!"

What—or rather who—was the slumbering dragon?

Kim dropped in the chair, and without planning to do so began to sort out the pieces of the golden dragon, turning over quickly those with the disturbing word on the back so he could no longer see it. This went here, that there, a five-clawed foot of an imperial dragon took shape. Then he had it all except one piece for the head—an eye on it. But the eye was closed, the dragon slept. Or did he? Was there the smallest hint of a raising lid? Did the dragon only pretend to sleep?

CHIN MU-TI

The light of the four lamps in the chamber was not enough to reach into the corners where shadows crouched. Chin Mu-Ti blinked and blinked again, fighting sleep. It was as if the Minister had forgotten him altogether and he was not to be dismissed this night to his pallet in the guards' hall. Though it was a great honor to be sword bearer and page to Chuko Liang, it was a wearing life, for the great one was ever restless and seemed never to feel weariness himself.

His master was looking from the window toward the distant mass of black hills. Somewhere in those hills Ssuma, Commanding General of Wei, led some twenty regiments of the enemy. Thinking about them, Mu-Ti felt a cold chill deep inside him, the marrow of his bones was close to melting. Ssuma's men were not to be driven lightly away, like autumn leaves by a wandering wind, nor would they disappear like March snows at the coming of the sun.

Once more he blinked sleepily, his eyes upon Chuko Liang's straight back. In these chambers the First Minister did not wear armor but rather the robe of a magistrate, his black cap stiff and straight upon his head. He was a spare man, with almost the leanness of one in famine time, tall as one of the trees on the distant hillsides.

Also he was one whose thoughts could not be read upon his face. But now all men knew what lay before them. And though Chuko Liang was one who drew ever from the well of wisdom, it was also true that no man may escape this shadow no matter how fast he runs— even though he be one of the three great heroes who have sworn a blood oath to the Emperor Liu Pei.

Though the Empire of Han had come on evil times and had been carved apart into thirds, yet all men knew that Liu Pei in truth was the Son of Heaven, of the House of Han, with the favor of the gods. There could not be two suns in the sky, let alone three, or three kings over the people.

Mu-Ti fought sleep with thought. What did they say of heroes? Their virtues—courage, justice, loyalty, mutual faith, truth, generosity, contempt for wealth—he listed them one by one in his mind. And, he remembered, courage itself was of three kinds. Courage in the blood: the face turns red when angry. Courage in the veins: the face turns blue. But courage of the spirit was the strongest of all: a man's face did not alter, only his voice strengthened in power, his eyes grew more piercing and—

One of the lamps, having exhausted its supply of gourd oil, flickered out. At the same time a hollow tramping sounded in the outer hall. Mu-Ti straightened to full attention as Chuko Lian came from the window. His was not a warrior's face, being thin and pale, with long drooping mustaches shading his mouth. He was more like a scholar than a man of action. Yet to the Son of Heaven he was both counseling head and fighting arm.

The dragon lies upon the sword; when the blade is raised the dragon makes war.

The generals Ma Su and Weng Ping had come in answer to their commander's midnight summons. They were in armor, their dragon helmets throwing demonlike shadows upon the walls, the bronze cheek pieces in the form of tiger's heads half concealing their faces. Ma Su's round, full jowls sprouted a closely cut fringe beard; his eyes glittered so that he seemed the war god from some frontier temple come to walk among men.

And he tramped ahead of his companion, as he was used to do in most company, pushing always before his fellow officers, his hand ever lying in show near the hilt of his sword. He was well read in the arts of war, which he let no man forget. From him was ever the first comment to come, as if he lived by the saying that to be heard afar one must beat a gong upon a hilltop. Yet he was a lucky leader of some skill, who had had his victories, though perhaps too many dead men paid for their general's reputation.

Mu-Ti watched him with hostility. It was well no thoughts could be read as they lay in the mind, or he would be in danger. But that his own father, Chin Fang, had paid with his life for a reckless sortie ordered by Ma Su, to no real gain, was graven on the boy's heart. Not that Ma Su knew or cared. What was a captain of mounted archers to a general of the forces? That was the measure of the man, for Chuko Liang would not have risked lives for show, neither would he thereafter have forgotten those who died.

"You have summoned us, Excellency?" Ma Su did not even wait for the Minister to speak, affecting the brusque manners of the soldier so eager in the service of the Emperor that he came running at summons, to stand with one foot in the stirrup ready to mount. Had he never heard that the mouth is sometimes a door leading to disaster?

Chuko Liang came in two long strides to the table on which still lay the message that had arrived less than an hour ago and the map he had been studying thereafter.

"Ssuma marches through the Hsieh Valley. If he succeeds he may easily pierce to the heart of Wu. This he must not do. Above all he must not take the Yangping Pass—" As he spoke the Minister stabbed here and there with his long forefinger on the surface of the map. He spoke abruptly, which was unusual—harshly, as if he could so make more quickly known to those who listened the full danger of what lay ahead.

"If the enemy reach Chiehting, they can block off all our needed supplies. Then all Shensi will lie open to them. We shall be forced back to Hanchung. They will cut roads, and with a month's starvation—" He made a gesture with those hands which seemed more fitted to grasp a writing brush than the hilt of the sword Mu-Ti now held scabbarded and upright, resting point down to the floor, its hilt between his palms.

"Ssuma is no fool: he knows we must at all cost prevent him doing this, lest our cause be ended here and now. Above all we must hold Chiehting. But let no man not understand that this is an act in which there is near ten-tenths of a chance that death waits—"

"We do not command an army of sword jugglers ready to show their skill at some festival, Excellency." Ma Su wrapped self-confidence about him as a thick cloak protecting against winter winds. "Not yet are the forces of Wu birds trapped in a net, or fish dumped into the cooking pot. Give me leave to march and Chiehting is as safe as if ten dragons loop their bodies around its walls!"

One of the Minister's slim hands rose; his fingers pulled at a drooping mustache end, rolled the long hairs between thumb and forefinger. Chuko Liang did not look at his general. Rather, his eyes were still on the map.

"Dragon begets dragon; battle, battle. Death and life are predetermined, riches and honor depend upon the will of Heaven. This city is small, but its value to us now is like the pearl in a sea oyster. You are deeply read in the rules of war, but strict defense is a different matter from the clash of swords, the thrust of spears, in open meeting with the enemy. There is no wall at Chiehting, no natural means of defense to work behind."

Ma Su shrugged. "Excellency, since I was a boy I have studied the arts of war. I am as well learned in those as a scholar in the sayings of the Revered Masters. Why should this defense be deemed so difficult by you, who know well what we have done in the past?"

"Mainly because Ssuma is no common general. Even

our own fingers are of unequal length and strength, and Ssuma is above eight-tenths of a leader. Also Chang Ho, who commands his van, is a man whose banners make others tremble, and with good reason."

"I have faced great leaders before, Excellency. Stout men, not stout walls, make a well-held city. This much do I wager on what I shall do at Chiehting—let it so be added to the roll of oaths: if I do not hold fast as you wish, then let my head be struck from my shoulders!"

Now Chuko Liang did look straight at him. And there was a hiss of breath from Weng Ping, who had not spoken.

"This is no hour for jesting. Keep such words for moments by the wine bowls—"

"I do not jest, Excellency. Let my oath be set down with brush and ink—placed in record, Weng here being witness."

"Jade and men are both shaped by harsh tools; be not unaware of sudden changes of fortune."

"Set it so, Excellency—that Ma Su shall hold Chiehting or else his head rolls!" There was a hot note in the General's voice, his full cheeks flushed.

"So will it be done. Now, I give you a legion and a half of men, and Weng Ping shall march with you. He is to use the care and caution for which he is known to all, and is to camp in the most commanding position so that the enemy may not steal by. Do not think small of Ssuma, he is the best the false Emperor has to serve him.

"When you are so set as to command the road by which the enemy must travel, then do you draw me a map of your defenses and all the local places to mark, and this must be sent to me. But above all—change not, nor add to, nor lessen from, these orders. And that when you go into battle you may not lack a single fighting man, my page here, Chin Mu-Ti, shall ride with you to be the map messenger when you have it ready for my hand."

"To speak is to have it done—" began Ma Su.

But Chuko Liang held up his hand to silence that formal acknowledgment of orders received, as he continued; "Northeast of Chiehting is the city of Liehliucheng, and near to that a hill path. Kao Hsiang will camp there in a stockade with a legion. If the threat to Chiehting becomes too great he will move to your assistance. Wu Yen will bring a troop to the rear of Chiehting as further reinforcements. Remember, you must take up your post on the most dangerous road to the Yangping Pass. Do not regard this all as idle talk, or make any move to spoil the plan."

"That is understood, Excellency." Ma Su saluted, tramping out of the chamber, Weng Ping again a stride behind. Mu-Ti had time only to lay the Minister's sword carefully on the table as he hurried to follow. He went reluctantly. Though Ma Su was not his commander, yet to be even so attached to his service for a time was galling, and he hoped he would not have to ride with him for long. As he left, he saw that Chuko Liang was again stooped over the map, studying its lines with fixed intensity.

Wei, Wu, Shu to the south: the Three Kingdoms into which the once great Empire of Han had split. In the dark days at the end of the dynasty, Liu Pei, though of the House of Heaven, had been so poor that he had made and sold sandals to earn food for his mother. Then the three great heroes—Kuan Yu, Cheng Fei, Chuko Liang—had sworn blood oaths to uphold him. Ts'ao Ts'ao wore the dragon gown in Wei, and Sun Ch'uan in the south. Much blood had flowed, many towns had been taken and burned, men had died in war, women and children had starved in summer, frozen in winter;

yet none of the Three Kingdoms had yielded one to the other. Truly this was a time when more sorrow than happiness, more shame than honor, governed the world of men.

Now, as Mu-Ti rode out through the night with Ma Su and his men, in the chill of the dark he lost some of his longing for sleep. He was a very humble member of the Generals' staff, riding at its tail, and so he could hear the muttering of men grumbling at the need for breaking their night's rest.

Once, from the dusky ranks of the foot soldiers, came words as the staff clattered by on horseback. "Ha, what do horsemen know of aching feet? Does mud care which cloak it bespatters?"

The guardsman at Mu-Ti's side cracked his whip threateningly at the unseen speaker. "Three inches of a never-idle tongue may well find itself shortened by two," he called back, though he must have already been well past the soldier who had so complained.

It was well into the following day before they reached the goal set them. Ma Su and Weng Ping and their men dismounted, ate cold oat cakes, and drank from saddle bottles. As he ate, Ma Su walked a little apart, staring about him critically at the looming hills and the road. Mu-Ti, his horse's reins looped about his wrist, ready to ride at the first command, moved closer to the two generals than the others. That he wore the First Minister's badge gave him, he decided, some freedom from the usual military custom in this company, and he somehow wanted to observe Ma Su, even as he fought the dragon's breath of hatred every time he looked upon him. Did he wish the General to fail? A thousand times yes, were it not that such failure would mean disaster for them all.

"I do not see why it is thought that Wei will dare to come into this place," Ma Su commented.

"His Excellency has had reports from the scouts sent to watch the march of the enemy. And he is one who thinks twice before he gives orders once."

"His Excellency's caution and farsightedness are well known." But there was a suggestion in Ma Su's tone that he did not altogether mean that statement to be a compliment. "Look to that hill standing there—look upon it closely, Weng Ping. It is well wooded, a heaven-created place to give one advantage over any man advancing along the road. Such a camp as the war god himself would choose above all others."

Weng Ping stared dutifully at the hill. Mu-Ti saw that he ran his tongue over his lower lip before he answered. To be a subordinate to such as Ma Su meant that the tongue must be guarded. Weng Ping well knew that the swiftest horse cannot overtake a word once spoken. "Elder brother," he said finally, "if we leave this road for the hill, and the forces of Ssuma then surround it, we are lost. Also, it was in the orders given me that I must set my men to felling trees to build a stockade fort right here."

Ma Su laughed. "Younger brother, it is easy to see you are not learned in the superior books of war. There it is stated as one of the major rules that one must strive to look down upon one's enemy from a higher position. If they attempt to march past here, I will swear that not even one of their breastplates shall be returned to him who sent them! Those who follow that part of themselves which is great are great men; those who follow that part which is little are little men."

And now Weng Ping flushed, for there was contempt in Ma Su's voice. Still he answered, and without any show of heat. "Perhaps that be true, elder brother. But have you noted that the hill lacks any spring of water and that the day is hot? If the enemy comes and captures the spring below those heights, what then? I bow to your superior learning in such matters, but also I have known thirst and it can move men strangely. Above all, this is not following our orders. Should we be blown east or west, when it was told us to do this and not that?"

"His Worthy Excellency Chuko Liang is not here. What does he know of this ground save what has been reported to him by scouts, doubtless ignorant men with no learning in the finer points of warfare? Were he here, he would agree with me straightway. As for the matter of water—desperate men fight desperately. Hungry barbarians will breach a city wall when the odor of prosperity within reaches their nostrils. If they thirst and must reach water, each man will fight as a hundred. Why do you, younger brother, presume now to oppose me? Am I not the commander here, one who has even given a blood pledge to be victor? Do you think I would risk my head were I not sure this is right and proper?"

"Give me a part of the force, then, to camp to the west below, that I may support you if trouble comes."

"You bark like a fox of ill omen." Ma Su puffed out his lips in a daunting scowl. "Why should I waste men so foolishly?"

But even as he spoke thus harshly there was a stir among the men waiting within bow shot. And their ranks opened to let through a man who stumbled and wavered as he ran. He wore the coarse clothing of a countryman, much stained and muddied, as if he had fallen often on soft, wet ground. He came to his knees before Ma Su, knocking his head against the earth in deep respect.

"What seek you here, fellow?" the General demanded.

"This worthless person brings a message to the Excellent and Honorable General. The army of the demon-commanded men of Wei is close. They come as fast as if they were mounted on air-flying dragons! Already their

162

scouts spy among the near hills, and behind them are as many as the locusts gathering to eat the crops of those Heaven has chosen to feel the weight of famine."

"Then it is time we prepare to meet them. A foot of jade is of no value, an inch of time is to be prized." The General spoke to those about him, but he gave no thanks to the one who had brought the warning. Instead he said directly to Weng Ping in a cold voice, "Since you have found it fit to question the rules of war, you shall take half a legion and do as you will with it. But in the hour of victory you must answer for your presumption."

"Elder brother, at that time I shall not seek to evade any questions which may be asked of me," Weng Ping answered. He called to his officers and messengers, ordering those spared to him by Ma Su to be ready to march. Also he beckoned to Mu-Ti, saying, "It is not forgotten that His Excellency desires a map to be taken to him. This I shall prepare for you."

Mu-Ti pushed to the side of the messenger, put a hand on the man's shoulder. The countryman, still breathing deeply, looked up. And Mu-Ti knew him, not as the countryman he seemed, but as one he had once seen at headquarters wearing the armor of a bowman. This was one of the "eyes and ears" of the forces. Mu-Ti brought out his saddle gourd and put the vessel in the spy's hands, saying, "Drink, elder brother."

But even as the other lifted it to his lips, he spoke over its rim. "Empty is the clear path to Heaven, crowded the dark road to Hell. When the mantis hunts the locust he forgets the shrike hunts him."

"Kao Hsiang camps at Liehliucheng with a legion." Mu-Ti could give no order, but the scout was a shrewd man. That statement would hold meaning for him.

He handed back the gourd, nodded, and slipped away. Ma Su's forces were already on the march toward the hill. But Mu-Ti, again in the saddle, followed Weng Ping.

His much smaller body of troops marched some distance from the hill where Ma Su's men now labored to cut down trees and build a rude fort. Then, on the road level, Weng Ping gave orders to do the same. While his men worked Weng Ping with his own hand copied on bamboo strips (those meant for the messages of first importance) a map of the country, marking the positions of his own force and that of Ma Su. He also made a short report of what the senior General had decided about a battleground. Then he wound the outer cover about the bundle of strips, sealing it with his thumb ring.

He summoned his own scouts and sent them to watch for the coming of Ssuma and the progress of Ma Su on the hill. But Mu-Ti left before they did, mounted on a horse selected for strength and speed, riding at a fast pace back to the headquarters of the army.

Twice he changed horses, but time moved also, and it was again late at night when he staggered reeling with weariness into the presence of Chuko Liang. The Minister took the message packet quickly from Mu-Ti, but he did not open it until he had ordered food and drink to be brought and had arranged that the boy himself be seated to have refreshment. He then read rapidly what Weng Ping had written, and the map he compared to the larger one still lying open on the table.

He glanced at Mu-Ti, who was chewing on an oil cake, trying to appease his inward-clawing hunger without too great loss of manners.

"From a gabled roof the rolling melon has two choices of descent, though both lead to disaster. A bad word whispered will echo a hundred miles. What you have seen and heard, do not repeat."

Mu-Ti put down the half-eaten cake. "This person is both blind and dumb, Lord."

But if he did not wish Mu-Ti to talk, Chuko Liang made no pretense of trying to spare his higher officers the full extent of possible disaster. And then those in the chamber saw what they never had seen before—Chuko Liang displaying anger. For he struck such a blow with his fist on the top of the table that the strong wood quivered. And he shouted in a voice which issued hotly from his throat, even as flames might issue from the maw of a dragon, "Now has Ma Su's ignorance and unworthy pride ruined the army! It is easy to enroll a thousand soldiers, but where does one find a good general?"

The officers in the room looked from one to another, gathering closer to their commander. And Yang I, who was of the highest rank there, dared to ask, "What is the dire thing which has happened, Excellency?"

"By this stupid disobedience of a direct order, perhaps we have already lost Chiehting, maybe even more. Ma Su wagered his head on this matter. Well, if he dies not in battle he will soon learn that a flaw in a scepter of jade may be ground away, but for a flaw in deed nothing can be done!"

Then Chuko Liang drew a cloak of calm once more around him. His hand went again to his mustache, twisting the hairs this way and that, which was always a sign he was in deep thought.

Yang I said then, "I am not too clever, or learned in the classics of war. But let me now replace Ma Su and perhaps all is not quite lost."

However, as the Minister nodded agreement, almost absently, and Yang I prepared to give orders to his men, there came another messenger, the first of many more.

Mu-Ti, dismissed at last to the comfort of his hard bed, did not hear the news which came, each time more dire, to be reported first to the Minister and then, from mouth to ear, mouth to ear, all through the fort. But when he was roused at last to attend his lord, he heard the whole of it. One man can be ordered tongueless, or two, but not six or seven.

Even as Weng Ping had warned, Ssuma's men surrounded the hill which Ma Su had chosen to fortify. Ssuma himself had ridden in disguise to view the station which the men of Wu had taken. But the brightness of the moonlight had made plain his face so that those in the stockade above had known him. And at that time Ma Su was reported to have laughed and said, "If he is well advised by fortune he will not attack us. The careless rat who chews upon the cats tail must be prepared for lightning."

Then Ma Su issued orders for his men to watch for a red flag to be raised at the hill's crown. When they saw that flag they were to attack. But in the meantime Ssuma's forces drew in closely, and the spring of water was now in enemy hands. Then another detachment of the forces of Wei moved on to check Weng Ping.

When the sun rose again, there was thirst among the men on the hill, which grew worse during the hottest hours of the day. Yet Ssuma made no move to attack, rather letting the heat of the sun work for him. And when at last Ma Su grew impatient and raised the flag, the men did not move forward. They were so heat-ridden in their armor that many were faint and fell gasping.

Ma Su, greatly angered, commanded that the officers in charge of the companies that had not moved were to be cut down where they stood for not obeying orders. When three or four had so fallen, the men indeed rose for a desperate sally downslope. Ssuma's men refused to meet them, greeting them from afar with a rain of well-aimed bolts from their crossbows. Then Ma Su ordered his men to withdraw to the stockade and to defend it until help came. But Weng Ping was so cut off he could not march to their relief.

Disorder broke out. Some of the men were angry because of their dead officers, others were mad for water. Some even surrendered that they might drink. And later the men of Wei set fire to the wood and brush on the hillside. Then at last Ma Su was driven to dash to the west, while Chang Ho, the leader of Ssuma's van, chased him into the camp of Wei Yen, well to the rear of Chiehting. A roll of signal drums halted that chase as Wei Yen's men in turn pushed the enemy back toward the city.

However, there Ssuma and his son had prepared an ambush for Wu Yen, and Weng Ping moved to save his comrades from being entrapped. While they fought so, their camps were overrun by fast-moving troops Ssuma had detached for that purpose, and they were driven back to the city of Liehliucheng, where Kao Hsiang came to their aid. They proposed a night attack, and so matters stood for awhile.

Wu Yen and the other commanders, determined to make sure of Chiehting, set out by three separate roads. But as they approached that city a bomb exploded in a brilliant light, drums rolled, and the enemy appeared demon-wise before them. Then, when Weng Ping reached the meeting place, they had to abandon their hope of retaking the city. They could only fight their way back to Liehliucheng, to discover Ssuma's men again before them.

Realizing that they were outnumbered as well as outgeneraled, Wu Yen suggested a retreat to retain the pass at Yangping. Part of Ssuma's army was pursuing them down the Chi valley, while the other half of the enemy forces, under Ssuma himself, was heading for Hsieh to capture there the main supply base and baggage train.

Thus they had already neared Hsicheng, a town which had another great depot of stores and which was also the only protection for the road leading to the important cities of Nanan, T'ienshin, and Aintiny.

Meanwhile, Mu-Ti, aroused from his slumber, had come back to the Minister's chamber. There were officers there, messengers coming and going. But he threaded his way through that throng and took up again the sword of Chuko Liang, ready to wait on his lord.

The Minister listened to the flood of ill reports, and now no expression of anger crossed his face. Nor did he hesitate, but gave swift orders to this man and that. And his armor bearer brought forward his armor, fitting it upon him even as he so spoke.

Across Mu-Ti's arm again rested the mighty battle sword. It had been a gift from the Son of Heaven himself, as one could see by the engraving on the blade when it was drawn. For there reared the five-clawed Lung of the Emperor. This differed from other dragons, for some trick of the artist's lines in drawing had partly lidded the huge eyes, so that the scaled protector seemed about to sleep, or else was but half awakened from some dream. Thus this blade was known as the "Slumbering Dragon."

When Mu-Ti brought it forward to the Minister, Chuko Liang, leaving it still in his page's hold, drew it forth a little from its scabbard and looked upon the dragon, his face still and set with purpose. "So it has all come to naught," he observed. "Mine is the fault. And when a fault is known it must be amended as well as such can be done. Each man follows the path of destiny, but no two paths are alike. It seems that mine now runs into a place of evil intent, wasted wisdom, and stupidity."

Then he called two captains of well-proven ability, Kuan and Chang, and he told them, "Take three companies of men and ride the road to Wukungshan. If you see the enemy, do not fight, but as you go beat your war drums, sound the horns of battle, and shout as loudly as might a great army. If they then retire, do not pursue, but ride directly for the Yangping Pass."

And he sent the commander Yang I to put all in the town of Chienko in order for retreat, gathering up the supplies and men, and the people living thereabouts who feared the coming of the enemy. Ma Tai and Chang Wei were to establish a rear guard, setting cunning ambushes along the valley.

All these orders he gave in a calm voice, as one who had a full year of time and was not in truth facing death and an end to all his planning. Nor did he neglect to send other riders to Nanan, T'ienshin, and Aintiny with the dark news that it might be well for those living there to take the road to Hanchung.

He was so calm that those who listened were heartened and armed with courage in turn, as if they had drunk deep of some stream wherein the war god himself had spilled his own wine of bravery. Then, with five companies, Chuko Liang took horse and they rode for Hsicheng to remove the stores there. For were those supplies to be taken or destroyed, it indeed would be a fatal blow to all the forces of Wu.

As they rode thus, Mu-Ti was directly behind his lord, carrying not the sword, which Chuko Liang had now taken into his own hand, but displaying the tailed banner of the Commander-in-Chief proudly and properly, that all might know Chuko Liang was such a leader as went into danger and not away from it. More messengers came, and always the news they brought was such as a man would not choose to hear—that Ssuma was sweeping toward them with a force to darken the country he passed over.

No leader of high rank was left with the Minister's own small troop save Chuko Liang himself, and some civil officials who were not fighting men. And when they reached the town after a forced march the Minister gave his orders sharply, right and left, so that men scattered and ran to do his bidding. Their already small company was halved, so that those men who were present to move the stores had to sweat and strain, getting them loaded on oxcarts to be drawn away from the doomed town.

But Chuko Liang left the scene of their frantic endeavors and himself climbed to the ramparts near the westward gate to see what lay before them. There was dust rising in great yellow clouds reaching to the very sky. Along two roads that dust hung, as if the jaws of a huge pincers were about to close on Hsicheng, finding the city an easy nut to crack.

The Minister watched only for a moment or two. Then again he made a stir with orders, using even Mu-Ti as his messenger. All the banners which had proclaimed the presence in Hsicheng of the forces of Wu were taken down as fast as men could pull them loose. The half-moon halberds of authority were dropped out of sight. And the word went forth through the whole city that no officer was to show himself, or make a sound, with death a quick penalty for disobedience.

Picked men unstrapped their armor, set aside their swords, spears, and crossbows, and put on the blue coats of peasants, so that they had the look of simple men. With brooms and cleaning baskets they set out in the streets to look like men whose business it was to make all tidy. Also, the foregate was loosed of its bars and pulled fully open, letting any who came see those streets clearly.

Meanwhile the Minister went to the gatehouse tower, where Mu-Ti helped him off with his armor, loosening the buckles and straps. He set aside the heavy dragon helm and his sword in its red lacquer sheath. In the place of all such war gear, Chuko Liang drew on an outer robe of gray, such as a simple Taoist priest might wear, and put on his head a black cap.

He summoned one of the youngest scribes, and to him he handed the pole of a yak-tail standard such as was carried for a magistrate. Mu-Ti, having put off his own light armor at the Commander's bidding, picked up the sheathed sword as was his duty.

Last of all the Minister reached for a lute, which he had sent Mu-Ti earlier to seek out in the town. He tested its stringing delicately, frowning a little as he made adjustments to his liking. Lute in hand, he went out on the parapet above the gate, where two of the soldiers had set a bench. And there he seated himself, the lute across his knees, the scribe and Mu-Ti taking their places, one on either side of him as if they were in some pleasant garden, come to enjoy the quiet of a summer afternoon afar from the clamor and danger of war.

Chuko Liang, having tuned the lute to his liking, began to play and sing one of the songs of Chi Kang:

"I will cast out wisdom and reject learning,
My thoughts shall wander in the great void—
Always repenting of wrongs done—"

Having finished that song, he began another. Yet never did he sing of war, but rather of the thoughts men held in times of peace, and those verses which had been written in quiet places.

Nor did he show the least interest in what was happening on the roads leading to the city. To the best of their ability Mu-Ti and the young scribe tried to copy his calm and lack of interest in their present surroundings.

What the scribe felt, Mu-Ti did not know. As for himself, he knew an inner shrinking, awaiting with a dread he fought hard to conceal the striking of the first crossbow bolts. For now the scouts of the enemy's van were riding below, though with the wariness of those suspecting ambush.

Then, having stared for a long moment at the open gates of the town and at the small party of three on the rampart, the scouts wheeled around and thundered back at a full gallop the way they had come. Mu-Ti grasped the sword tighter, as if holding it so, even sheathed, could afford some defense. But Chuko Liang smiled gently as he finished his song, only to begin another, this time voicing words in praise of wind-driven clouds.

Instead of the scouts, a party of officers now returned. And judging by their rich armor, they were of high rank, though they carried no name banner. Close to the wall they wheeled around and halted, and there they sat in their saddles for a period which seemed to Mu-Ti to be very long indeed. They listened to Chuko Liang as if the light words he sang carried some dire meaning, yet now he praised leaves driven by the autumn breeze. Nor did he take any notice of those below, but fixed his gaze well above their heads, as if they were ghosts without power to be seen.

Mu-Ti watched them speak to one another. One even rode closer to look within the gates along that street where men walked and swept in seeming unconcern.

That man of Wei rode back to his companions, and now he seemed to urge some course upon the most richly armored of the party. But at length the officer threw up his hand in a gesture of sharp command and they all turned to gallop away. The Minister sang on as once more dust arose. Only this time it signaled the retreat of the force of Wei. Mu-Ti drew a deep breath of wonder.

Then Chuko Liang laughed aloud and put aside the lute of clap his hands, while out of the tower came some of the civil officials who had ridden with his staff.

"Excellency, what magic have you wrought?" the eldest dared to ask. "Did you sing some spell written by the Sages that this was done?"

Again the Minister laughed. "No magic did I use, younger brother. Unless knowing a man's way of thought is magic. There is an old saying, 'Beware the Slumbering Dragon, stir him not awake.' Ssuma thought that he saw here a slumbering dragon, such as that set upon my sword—caution kept him from waking it. He knows well my reputation for never doing anything not ten times thought upon, that I play not recklessly with danger. Thus, when he saw the open gates inviting him into the town, he suspected an ambush cleverly laid. When he saw me at my ease, playing upon a lute, my hand reaching for its strings rather than the sword hilt, he believed I must be so safe that I need not actively defend myself. Now he will retire, and in so doing he will meet the able Kuan and Chang already in position to give him a sharp lesson. But—had I been in his place, I would not have turned aside. He will long have reason to regret this day."

Then once more the Minister became a man of swift action, giving orders that the town be speedily cleared of the remainder of the supplies, and that those and its people be escorted to Hunchung. For he knew that Ssuma would not be long in returning.

But the words he had spoken had already passed among the soldiers and then to the people of the town. So as he rode out among them they hailed him as "Slumbering Dragon."

It was later that Ma Su was brought to him. And seeing the Commander he had disobeyed, the General threw himself down upon the ground, beating his forehead against the earth, begging mercy. But though Chuko Liang looked with pity on the humbled man, he said:

"When Heaven sends calamities it is possible to escape; when one occasions the calamity himself it is no longer possible to live. It is truly said that the mouth is a door leading to disaster; no less is it certain that by impatience and folly may great plans be brought to ruin. If the first words of an order fail, ten thousand will not then prevail. And no man may call himself a soldier unless he obeys the order of his leader.

"You rashly swore victory or your head, pledging this by solemn oath. Then you threw away victory, being led by the demon of pride to question the worth of carefully thought out plans. Upon your head now falls the fate you yourself asked."

So they dealt with Ma Su even as he had, in his great conceit, suggested that they do. But Chuko Liang knew him to be a brave man with no treachery in him, only stupid with pride. So he did not allow the family of Ma Su to suffer, rather took them into his own household.

But also, at the first interval when he had time, the Minister gathered together his senior officers and showed them the report of all that had happened, which he had written out to be sent to the Son of Heaven. To this report, which ended with the account of the execution of Ma Su, he had added these words:

"He who selects the wrong man for a post of danger is himself in grave error. This person is no longer fit to be one trusted by the Throne. Therefore those undeserved honors and awards which have been given in the past to this unworthy servant, the position he holds, must rightfully be taken from him. And in addition he must be fittingly punished for the wrongs he committed in the ill use of power."

Though his officers protested loudly, Chuko Liang would change none of these words in which he resigned as First Minister Thus the report was sent to be put into the hands of the Emperor.

At first the Emperor protested. But Chuko Liang held firm in his resolve and insisted that he was no longer fit for his post, having made such a fatal error as to select Ma Su as chief commander in the field. The Emperor honored such honesty, which held by the teachings of older, more upright days. So, though he took away the post of First Minister, still he laid upon Chuko Liang the generalship of the army, with as many rights and duties as he had held before, only the outer honor being lessened. And all men continued to speak highly of Chuko Liang as a wise and honorable man.

And they made the Slumbering Dragon a subject of song, which said to him:

"Quite open lay the city to the foe,
But Chuko's lute of jasper wonders wrought
It turned aside the legion's onward march
For both leaders guessed the other's thought."

6

DUST ON THE TABLE

"Slumbering dragon"—the words sighed through the dark room hissingly, as if the dragon himself had spoken them.

But the dragon slept upon the table, his eyes half shut. He looked just like the one on Chuko Liang's sword. That had been silver, though, because it was on a steel blade, whereas this one was the Imperial Yellow, as it might appear on the Son of Heaven's own banner.

The Son of Heaven! It was a long, long time since there had been an Emperor in China. Kim ran his finger-tip lightly over the body of the yellow dragon. The pieces had gone so tightly together he could hardly see or feel their divisions now. The puzzle was complete.

Dragons—he studied the silver one coiling at the top, the queer blue one at the bottom, the red to balance the yellow at the sides. Had they—Sig, Ras, Artie—also met dragons?

But Shui Mien Lung held him the longest. Kim could feel again that weariness that had struck to his very bones when he had ridden with Ma Su and Weng Ping and then returned with the map and the report. He also knew again the fear that had dried his mouth, yet made his hands sweat on the hilt of the sheathed sword as he stood beside the Minister and watched Ssuma and his officers ride up to the wall.

You made no excuses, you took the blame for your errors of choice as well as act. That was what he had learned from Chuko Liang. Whole sentences the Minister had said came back to him word by word.

What had Kim been doing these past days since he had moved here, gone to the new school? When he had felt lost and alone he had made it the school's fault for being too big, too full of strangers, his parent's fault for moving—everyone's but his own. No one was going to hunt him out, beg him, Kim Stevens, to be a friend. He could continue to wark in error, believing he was right, as Ma Su had done—or he could follow the path of the Slumbering Dragon.

Chuko had used his wits and taken triumph out of defeat. There were different ways to face the future: like Chuko, like Ma Su. And now he knew which he would try. Suddenly, for a moment or two he was Mu-Ti again, folding his hands together in a way which seemed right and proper, bowing his head respectfully to the yellow dragon.

"A thousand, thousand thanks, Great and Noble One," he said in the Hong Kong speech he had not used for a long time now. "That you have kindly shown this unworthy one the rightful path is a great honor. May this one continue to walk in it hereafter." For the second time he bowed to the dragon as Chin Mu-Ti would have done.

Then he took his book bag and started out of the dusky room. How long had he lived in that dream? An hour—two? Mother would be worried. Kim had seen her watching him with that shadow in her eyes these past days. She and Father both had asked him about school, how he liked it. And several times Mother had suggested that he ask home some school friends as he used to bring James Fong and Sam Lewis. He had not known just how to answer without letting her guess how he hated it all. Now, as Chuko Liang had done, he would face fear. And though he did not play the lute or sing in the face of the enemy, he would do what he could.

Kim ran through the dark rooms, climbed out the kitchen window, shutting it behind him. Then he halted on the porch. The puzzle! If someone was coming to clear out the house what about the puzzle? It would be taken away!

Yet he did not want to go back alone to get it. Sig, Ras, and Artie—they all had a part of it. He ought to talk to them first, ask what should be done. Suppose he stopped at Sig's house, they might still be there—

Kim glanced at his wrist watch, a birthday present two months ago. Twenty minutes to five! But he had gotten off the bus at four fifteen—he had been here only about half an hour! Days had passed in the dream, half an hour in real time. Still, twenty to five was later than usual. And now, at all times, he did not want to worry mother.

He could see the boys later. Better yet, he thought, suppose he called them all up, asked them over? If they could come, then they might decide about the puzzle, maybe collect it from the house together after school tomorrow. Kim put on an unusual burst of speed, running down the street, his book bag thumping against his leg, very eager to get to the phone and make those calls. In one way it would be the first battle in his own private war, his first chance to prove that he could follow Chuko Liang's example.

Mother herself was using the phone when Kim came into the house. He could see her sitting on the edge of the couch, listening. She smiled and waved, pointing to the kitchen, where he knew there would be cookies and milk waiting. He hung his jacket and cap in the closet, set his book bag on the bottom stair, to be taken to his room later. But this time he did not take his library book out to read while he ate. What he had to think about was far more exciting than anything he could read, he was sure of that.

There were two brownies on the snack plate, and the rest of the kitchen had a good smell. Then he remembered about the bake sale at church. Mother must have promised to make a lot of things for that. He could see two covered cake tins and a couple of big pans with foil pinched over their tops. Nobody could bake like Mother. Kim nibbled around the edge of the first brownie to make it last.

"Well"—Mother stood in the kitchen doorway—"how did it go today, Kim?"

"All right. Please, could I ask some of the boys over maybe after supper? They live close—Sig, he's down on Ashford, and Ras and Artie are close—"

"This is a school night and there's homework, isn't there?"

He nodded, his mouth was full of brownie, too full to let him answer politely as he should. Then he swallowed fast.

"This is special. And it wouldn't take very long." He hesitated, knowing that Mother would wonder what was so special and why he did not tell her all about it.

But she did not ask any questions, which was one of the best things about Mother.

"If their parents say they may come, why, yes, Kim. Maybe for a half-hour or so. But on school nights—"

"Yes," he agreed. Rules were rules and he had never asked to change them before. But this *was* important. Suppose they came to clean out the old house tomorrow and the puzzle was gone! Could he leave for school earlier tomorrow without having to say why, get the puzzle safely out on the way to school? Or if he could not, might one of the others?

In one bite he ate the rest of the brownie and went to

look up phone numbers, taking them alphabetically so that Ras—George Brown—was first. With luck Ras himself answered.

Kim had not thought out ahead of time what to say, and now he fumbled for the right words. After all, Ras did not know, could not know, that he had been working the puzzle, too.

Also, it was not very helpful when he said, "This is Kim" to have Ras say, "Kim who?"

"Kim Stevens. I wait at the bus stop with you."

"Sure." But there was such a note of bewilderment in Ras's voice even now that Kim was discouraged. He could only hurry on and hope for the best, though he was a little afraid that the other boy would not listen to him.

"I know—about the dragons. I—I put together the yellow one this afternoon!"

For a long minute there was no answer at all. Kim felt almost as cold inside as he had on the wall of that long-ago city. Was Ras going to be angry with him, or even hang up? The silence stretched very long indeed before the other said, "Something happened to you, didn't it?"

"Yes! And, Ras, what about it—the you-know-what—if they come to clear out the house? Could—could you come over after supper and talk about it? Maybe even if we wait until tomorrow it will be too late."

"I'll have to ask. What about Sig—Artie?"

"I'm going to call them."

Ras went away from the phone to come back with a promise of "after supper for sure." Kim had been looking up Sig's number in the book, had his finger under it ready for the second call. And he had luck when he reached Sig, for Artie was still there, so he got them both and gathered two more promises.

When they arrived he was waiting impatiently. Father

183

had the TV on to listen to the news, and Mother was back on the phone talking about the bake sale, so he took them straight up to his room. Sig and Artie sat on the bed, looking about them with open curiosity. Ras had the desk chair, but Kim stood, eager to begin.

"You've got a groovy place." Sig studied the shelves up on the wall, holding the things Father had brought back from Hong Kong and Japan and Korea. "Hey—look—there's a dragon!"

He pointed to a wood carving.

"That's from Taiwan," Kim said impatiently.

"Looks a lot like the yellow dragon on the box lid." Sig got up and went to inspect it more closely.

Kim shook his head. "The yellow dragon is a Lung, one belonging to the Emperor."

"How can you tell?" Artie wanted to know.

"First, because it is yellow, that's the color that only the Emperor could wear or use. Then, it had five claws on its feet, that makes it a Lung. But the one in the puzzle is Shui Mien Lung—that means 'Slumbering Dragon,' and it was not really a dragon but a man—a man who lived in China a long time ago. He was First Minister and General-in-Chief to the Emperor Liu Pei, and he had a sword the Emperor had given him with a closed-eyed dragon engraved on it. Then he did something big and brave and the people called *him* Slumbering Dragon —they even made up a song about him—" Kim talked faster and faster, glad to see he had their full attention now and that they seemed to believe all he said.

"A man, not a dragon." Artie nodded. "Mine was, too —Artos Pendragon—he was a king and *he* had an important sword. But his dragon wasn't on the sword, it was a big red banner. When the wind filled it, it looked like a dragon flying."

"Mine was a real dragon—or once it had been a man

184

and then it became a dragon—but it was bad. It had to be killed. They called it Fafnir. Sigurd King's-son killed it with the sword Balmung. Odin helped him—" Sig contributed.

"Sirrush-Lau was real, too," Ras cut in. "It was horrible—like a big snake mixed up with an alligator, or one of those prehistoric monsters. The priests of Marduk-Bel kept it in a pool in the temple and they were going to have it kill Daniel, only he figured out a way to kill it first."

Kim's head turned from one to the other as he listened eagerly. So he had been right in his guess that each had had a dragon, as different as the four pictures on the cover of the box. And he wanted to know more, all of what had happened to each of them. Pendragon, Fafnir, Sirrush-Lau—strange names. But probably to Sig, Artie, and Ras "Shui Mien Lung" sounded just as queer.

"The puzzle"—he brought them back to the immediate problem. "What's going to happen to it if they come and take everything out of the house, maybe tomorrow?"

"You put the yellow dragon together, finished it this afternoon?" Ras wanted to know.

Kim nodded.

"Then you left it there on the table?"

"Yes. I thought it was late, that Mother would worry. Then—then I guess I just never thought of taking it apart. You know, it was so tight I couldn't even see the cracks marking the pieces, or feel them."

"We can't go after it tonight." Sig was walking from the bed to door and back again, as if he could think better when he was on the move. "Not tonight. At least I couldn't get away to try that. I can't even stay long here, the folks were talking homework when I left."

Ras and Artie were nodding in complete agreement.

"So we'll just have to leave it until after school tomorrow and hope that they don't come to clear things out before then. But we'll go after it together—after school—agree on that, you guys?"

They answered "yes," almost together. Then Sig turned to Kim. "We want to hear your story, all of it. Maybe we haven't much time tonight, but tell us what you can."

So Kim began to talk, trying to make vivid to them the mistake of Ma Su, the cleverness and courage of Chuko Liang. However, there was a lot he feared he could not make them understand. When he had done Ras was leaning forward, staring at Kim, as if he saw not the other boy at all but rather what he had been describing. And Sig, back on the bed beside Artie, and Artie himself were spellbound.

"That Ma Su"—Ras spoke first—"was he ever stupid! Bet his head on being right and then went out and proved how wrong he was!"

"I don't understand—really—why Chuko Liang thought *he* had been wrong and why he wanted to give up everything," Artie said slowly. "He—he really beat this Ssuma, didn't he? And did it without fighting, too. Why did he say he had failed? Oh, I know what you say he said, that he made a mistake in picking the wrong guy for the job, so he was responsible. But that's being pretty hard on himself—at least I think so."

"It was the way they believed, the old Chinese." Kim tried to make it clear. "They had a code they had to live up to. A lot of men didn't, but the heroes tried the hardest and sometimes they did."

"Yes," Sig broke in. "Like Sigurd refusing to touch the treasure even when he had a right to it, after he killed Fafnir! He knew the treasure changed the man who took it, as it did Mimir, so he wouldn't touch it."

"What happened to Sigurd?" Kim demanded.

"A lot, but I won't have time to tell you tonight," Sig answered. "Tomorrow—listen, we went to the library today and we got some books. Me, I got a second one about Sigurd, not exactly the same story—Sig Clawhand wasn't in it at all. That was me—Sig Clawhand—I was with Sigurd when he went to kill Fafnir, before that, too. And Ras, he got a book about Egypt, but there's nothing about Meroë in it, so he has to get another one and keep on looking. Artie—he got a good one—about the real Arthur, not the King with the Knights and the Round Table and all that stuff. Now—maybe you can find out something about this Chuko Liang. If our heroes are real, then yours must be also!"

"And when we come home tomorrow we'll all go together and get the puzzle." Ras stood up.

Upon that they agreed and the three left. Kim went back to sit down at his desk and open his book. There was homework waiting. But it was very hard to concentrate on anything between the covers of a book now. He wanted to know all Sig could tell him about Fafnir, all Artie could about Pendragon, all Ras could report of the monster Sirrush-Lau—and to wait was hard. In fact, he was not sure as he closed his last book that he had really accomplished very much studying that evening.

"Those seemed very pleasant boys," Mother commented at breakfast. "I am so glad you have found some new friends, Kim. Starting in at a new school as large as Anthony Wayne is hard enough, but to have to do it alone makes it worse. I know Mrs. Dortmund, and I have seen Mrs. Jones and Mrs. Brown at P.T.A. meetings. They all live so close"—she did not finish her sentence, but Kim guessed that she meant she was not worried so much any more about Kim liking the new house and neighborhood.

But he was impatient to get to the bus stop, so he hurried faster than he had in days to get out of the house and down the street.

"Hey! Wait up, man!" Artie's voice was loud and Kim slowed as the other came down his walk still zipping up his jacket. They picked up Ras at the next corner and Sig halfway down the block, arriving at the stop all together.

There were no signs of life around the old house. But it was early, only seven thirty, and if the Good Will came to clean the place out it would probably be later.

"I sure wish this was Saturday!" Artie said.

"Well, it isn't!" Ras answered him. "And we'll just have to hope they won't get here today."

"We got about ten minutes maybe," Artie urged. "Why can't we sneak in and get it now?"

"With all of these hanging around to see us?" Sig pointed to the little kids, as well as two mothers who had escorted their own children and were waiting to see them safely on the bus.

They agreed gloomily that he was right. So they used the time to fill Kim in on their own adventures, until he got the accounts rather mixed, with all the interruptions of one or another who suddenly remembered something he just had to add, cutting into the middle of somebody else's story to do it.

That Tuesday was the second longest school day Kim could remember—almost as long as the day before had been, when he had wanted to find out what the other boys were doing in the house. It dragged so that each period seemed to last about four weary hours. And when he finally climbed into the homeward-bound bus it was with the feeling that he had spent about a week cooped up in classrooms and halls.

He had had three classes with Artie, Sig, and Ras. And Ras and he had had the same lunch period and so managed to get seats together. But they dared not say too much about what was uppermost in their minds for fear someone would overhear. It was a relief to be homeward bound and know they could get to the puzzle soon.

But the closer they came to their corner, the more they worried about what had happened in their day-long absence. Had the Good Will come and cleaned out the house? Kim really felt quite desperate as the bus swung around to let them off.

As one they turned to face the overgrown garden.

"No trucks here now, anyway." Artie gave a sight of relief.

"That doesn't mean anything," Ras pointed out. "They could have come and gone. We won't know until we get inside."

"Take it easy," Sig warned. "We have to go under cover, behind these bushes, and keep out of sight. Don't want anyone to see us and ask questions. But snap to it once we're in!"

They ran, obeying his instructions, putting a screen of bushes between them and the open gate. Then they reached the back porch, Sig in the lead. He pushed up the window to slip inside, Artie nudging him along so he could follow faster.

"I don't think they've come yet," Sig heartened them as they entered. "All the kitchen stuff is still here."

The same was true in the dining and living rooms. It did not take long to reach the puzzle room. But Sig stopped short inside the door, and Artie, Ras, and Kim pushed against him to get in themselves. A moment later they saw what had halted him.

There was the table and the chair. But the top of the table was bare. There was no completed puzzle of shining pieces, no glitter of color. Not even the box remained. There was nothing but the chair and the table, and a lot of dust, and a great many spider webs.

"I—I left it right here." He tapped the tabletop with his finger. Then he stared down in complete amazement, just as Sig had shown at the door.

"It's not here now," Sig was saying. But Ras had moved over to Kim and stood watching him.

"What is it, man? What's got you bugged?"

"Dust!" Kim pointed. "Look at all the dust! See, that's where I just touched—I made a mark. But all the rest—it's thick with dust! How—how could the puzzle have been here? How could we have shoved all those pieces around and not brushed the dust away?"

Ras leaned closer. "Hey, look here, you guys—he's right! There's sure a lot of dust. And you don't get that much dust, even in an old place like this, just overnight. Even if someone took the puzzle away last night, there wouldn't be all this dust on the table. Look, I can even write my name on it!"

And with a fingertip he printed G-E-O-R-G-E on the table's surface.

"But," Artie protested, his voice shrill, "I *know* it was right there—on that table! I saw it there—there was the silver dragon, and the blue one, and the red I worked—and a lot of yellow pieces—and the box—all right there!" He put down a finger in turn, stirring up more dust.

"I saw it"—Sig slowly nodded his head—"and so did you, Ras. And Kim was after us, he worked the last dragon. I know he didn't make up that story—it fits. A different dragon, but the story was like ours. And we all know ours were true. But—the puzzle is gone—and the box—and all that dust— It just doesn't make sense!"

"Maybe," Kim said—he had been trying to think straight ever since he had come to the empty table—"maybe we weren't supposed to keep the puzzle. Maybe it was only meant to be worked once."

"But why?" Artie asked the question none of them could answer.

"Who knows?" was the best Ras could say. "Just this—I *know* what I saw, though it may be gone now. And I know what I did when I was Sherkarer of Meroë. Even if the puzzle is gone I am going to remember that."

"Yes, and maybe Kim's right," Sig said. "Maybe we each were to have only one chance at the puzzle, and we had it."

"But the dust—where did the dust come from?"

"How do we know? That old guy—the one who used to live here—he got queer things from all over the world. Maybe there was something extra queer about the puzzle—"

"Do you mean *magic?*" demanded Artie. "Magic—that's silly, nobody believes in that but little kids."

"Something like magic," Kim returned firmly. "You've heard of mind reading, things like that. There was that TV program they showed last month—the one about people who knew about things happening a long way off at the same time they were happening. It doesn't need to be the storybook kind of magic, it could even be a kind of magic, it could even be a kind of science we don't understand yet. Look here—I'm Chinese, so I have an adventure back in Chinese history. You, Sig—what country did your people come from originally?"

"Granddad was German."

"So—you have an adventure in Germany. And Ras—he has one in long-ago Africa, and Artie—did your people come from England?"

"Wales."

"Well, Wales is part of old Britain. So we may just be living over things that happened to our great-great-great—about a thousand times back—grandfathers. That makes a kind of sense, doesn't it? Anyway, the puzzle is gone—but Ras is right, we can keep remembering what happened to us. Maybe that was what was meant to happen, that we could remember."

Artie was already on his way to the door. "No use staying here any more," he said a little too loudly. "I don't like the feel of this place now."

He only put into words what the others sensed. The room which had once welcomed them now pushed them out, the house wanted to get rid of them. They hurried through its rooms to obey an order they had felt though not heard.

"I wonder where it went—the puzzle," Sig said.

"We'll never know," Ras answered. "But I think Kim's onto something—maybe we did have great-great-greats who did those things we did. And—I'm sure glad I had a chance to fit together Sirrush-Lau!"

Even Artie could only nod "yes" to that. He was not sure about what Kim had said. But—he wished it were true—he liked to think that Artos, son of Marius, namesake of the High King, was a great-great-great who had lived somewhere far back in time. Artos was *real!*

Sig flexed his hand. It was not pulled into any claw. But he could remember how it had been once—Sig Clawhand—Sig Dortmund—there was a tie there, he knew it.

Kim heard a rustling of the dead leaves through which they were tramping. But he marched to something else—the drums of Chuko Liang's small, beleaguered army. He swung his book bag and for an instant or two he could almost believe its weight to be that of a sword in a red lacquer sheath.